Also by Sheila Solomon Klass

Novels
Come Back on Monday
Bahadur Means Hero

Memoir
Everyone in this House Makes Babies

Young People's Novels
Nobody Knows Me in Miami
To See My Mother Dance

A Perpetual Surprise

Sheila Solomon Klass

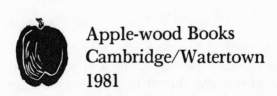
Apple-wood Books
Cambridge/Watertown
1981

Acknowledgment

The author wishes to thank the Yaddo Corporation for its hospitality and encouragement during the writing of this work.

A Perpetual Surprise © 1981 Sheila Solomon Klass

ISBN: 0-918222-29-X

A Perpetual Surprise

For
Perri Elizabeth
Tulsi Devi Klass
Child of Felicity

*That I exist is a perpetual surprise
which is life.*

—Rabindranath Tagore
Stray Birds XXII

Prologue

About two hundred kilometers north of Calcutta as the *kak** flies, is the industrial district of Asansol, the only area in the world where people breathe a colorful, odorful substance and not a gas. The air there is so thick it is visible; one can taste it and smell it and touch it.

Occasionally, when an Asansolee lights a match to start his dung-cake fire, he inadvertently sets the atmosphere ablaze. Such a combustion is easily extinguished by throwing a cloth around that portion of the ozone that has been ignited. Only once did a newcomer to the region, one Robi Gangulee, start such a conflagration and find himself unable to stop it. He owned only a single *dhoti*, a miserable cotton rag which covered his loins, and he could not bring himself to use this garment. His arsonous modesty threatened the entire town.

Fortunately, another immigrant, a pragmatic Nepali, Bahadur by name, happened to be cheating at cards on the road nearby, and he came to the rescue with his bedcover, a handsome muslin sheet with *CALCUTTA HILTON* embroidered on it in elegant Sanskrit characters.

Asansol was saved! The two lone men went their separate ways unaware that their lives had been melded by the force that created that fire.

---

*crow, what else?

Robi Gangulee, refugee, was not to be blamed for the hazards of his new environment. Thousands of poor men, much like him, today wander the same roads seeking work. Alas, there is more coal in the air of Asansol than there is in the fields; local resources are null and void, and the ground is sinking. All the countryside is a moon, barren, pocked with craters and piled with shale.

During the day the inhabitants enjoy the unique solar heat which may be depended upon for a consistent 100 degrees Fahrenheit. Evenings there is the lush apricot glow from the blast furnaces of Durgapur tinging the night with flame orange, dusty pink, and volcanic red. The only thirty-third-degree Mason in all of Asansol has been overheard boasting to visiting Masons as he clasped them in his arcane painful grip, that this was "... the single region in the whole world that offered *pollution in technicolor!*" These were his very words and thirty-third-degree Masons do not lie!

The illustrious Delhi government is fond of officially noting the similarity between Asansol and the great industrial valley of Germany. Acting on this cue, the Service Clubs of the district—led by this same Mason—held a public ceremony in 1957 marking the tenth year of national independence, during which they erected a proud white metal sign on the lightpost, just where the Grand Trunk Road debouches into town. The sign, now bent and rusted remains nevertheless for all to read:

"ASANSOL—INDIA'S RUHR"

The reasoning behind this sign is, if a place is grandly called, that is how it will be pictured in the mind's eye.

Thus the blind son's name is always Lotus-eyed.

"Robi Gangulee is not a coolie! No matter what life does to him, he is not a coolie!" He recited this credo to himself over and over as he trotted back and forth all day long, back and forth pulling lower caste *babus*, those Hindu gentlemen whose bellies were so bloated with curried goat meat and rice and chutney they would have done better to walk. Exercise is most salubrious, the *Veda* advises.

This low position, hauler of men and merchandise, burned Robi's unshirted back and scorched his soul as he ran on the open tar road.

"Robi Gangulee may be a ricksha-wallah but he is not a coolie!" He would fling this defiance at his detractors, evenings, at the small adobe-walled tea shops on Khudapur Road.

"Tell us about it, Robibabu," some habitué could always be counted on to urge. The nightly story served the way a favorite phonograph record does, as familiar entertainment for the regular road people and as a curiosity for new arrivals. Furthermore, Robi was literate, so that after the crowd heard him out, they could prevail upon him to read aloud from the day's Bengali newspaper borrowed from the Postmaster.

He reviewed for them, at length, the injustices of life, like a *B.A. Failed,* savoring each trial on the raw tongue of memory then spitting it out. As the rich man fondles his rupees, so Robi repeatedly probed his injuries but with much more pleasure.

"When I was younger," he lectured the assembled louts squatting together on the broken macadam road around the outside hearth, "I kept my head busy with *Gita*; this made me forget my hunger and guided my mind upward toward higher aspects. I sang away discomfort by chanting sweet *mantras* and offered my best to the gods, to Krishna, Kali Ma, Ganesh, and Blessed Saraswati, Mother of Knowledge. I designed these mental activities to console myself and to keep from dwelling on my cramps, those knots of hunger that locked tighter in my belly than the locks on the nearby grocer's go-down..." He dammed the flood of words and stood silent, his severe face bathed in the melancholy of his memories.

"What happened, Robibabu? What happened?" his listeners demanded.

"The hunger blew bigger than a child's balloon until one night it exploded the locks of the go-down and I enjoyed rice luxurious, ill-gotten but sweet so sweet." He conjured up the mythic rice.

Sounds of pleasure came from many throats. "Tell us more," they urged, but he was near to weeping at his own sad tale. He reached for the crumpled newspaper, smoothing it so that he could begin to scan it and tell the bad news that had happened that day to *other* men all over the world. It would give him comfort.

Robi's family were pure Sylhet Brahmins who were forced to flee at the birth of Pakistan like mice before a crazed cat. The Motherland, India, absorbed them and made them welcome, and then, when they were settled and beginning to prosper, she breathed an unkind breath over them—malaria.

His worthy parents, learned in herbs and medicinal teas, doctored themselves. They did all the traditional and proper things; first they took five, then seven, then nine live bugs with betel leaves on three successive days. This is the classic cure for chills accompanied by fever.

Alas, during the course of the classic cure, they died.

Malaria does not just casually visit; it is like an unwelcome relative who moves in and lays siege and waste to all. At such a time, the wisdom of the Sages is as nothing before the decision of the gods.

These were his beginnings, and from their unvarying pattern a Universal Law may be discerned: *Once Robi Gangulee was forced by Fate to be a ricksha-wallah, every bullock using the road immediately contracted diarrhea.*

As he moved along the filthied highway, pulling the ricksha, a rusted nail lodged itself in the tender valley between his toes. He was convinced that the Grand Trunk Road had been designed by the British Dalhousie Demon to torment him by running uphill in both directions, with crude stalagmites alternating with glass splinters to make up the macadam.

His passenger, a *Babu* with a big belly, shouted that Robi must stop at once. The passenger needed to relieve himself, Robi understood. Only the urgency of Nature's Call could make a man so frantic.

Robi resolved to tease Nature for a bit, to make his feet move even more swiftly while he feigned deafness. He would not halt until the passenger addressed him courteously. "Stop, coolie—" The churl was shouting. "Stop, Boy!"

Robi was no *boy*. Only one week before, he had looked at himself in the apothecary's mirror and noted that he had gray hairs. "Death's cards of invitation" Tagore had called them, when writing about an aging king. Gray hairs came early to aristocrats. Baser folk had hair that kept its blackness; it matched their sins.

Robi ran faster than he had ever run before, spurred on by his proud thoughts. Peeking back over his shoulder, he saw the protesting man's voluminous white clothing blowing in the wind, like the sails of the clipper ship on the calendar in the tea shop. Robi sweetened his voice now with the syrup of concern. "Yes, *Babu?* What is the difficulty?"

"I am thirsty and I wish a sweet drink."

"Indeed, it is a very warm day," Robi agreed amiably. "I too am parched and hot."

"I called to you to stop at the shop we passed back there, coolie."

"But that was merely a country shack, sir," Robi argued, "a dump, not fit for a customer like yourself."

"That is where I wanted to stop."

"Another shop is just ahead, your honor," Robi advised. "A much better shop is just around the bend in the road."

"I have no interest in another shop."

"Patience, sir. A very few minutes in this direction will take us to a first-class shop, not a shack like the one we passed."

"My father's younger brother is the proprietor of that *shack!*" the passenger shouted. He complexion was pomegranate-colored with anger.

"Ai—sir —" Robi's voice faltered. "I did not know."

"Family is all. That much you do know, eh, coolie?"

"Yes, sir. but since we have already long passed your uncle's modest—"

"You wish to be paid for this journey?" The passenger was brusque.

"I must be paid."

"Then take me back to my uncle's shop."

Robi sighed. *"Babu, we are now returning."*

That was his birthright. Coolies got passengers who gave handfuls of coins in tips. His passengers thirsted for drinks in shops already passed. To look at him, no one would believe that he could read and write Sanskrit, Hindi and Bengali, that his father had owned fifteen acres of farmland and his own well of sweet water. With a bullock to walk round and round and draw the water. In his father's house, rice was as plentiful as—rice!

He who had once won first honors in school and had studied almost until he had the down of manhood fuzzing his chin, was now clad only in the torn *dhoti* which he laundered upon himself in the pond, for he had no other garment. A ripped undershirt for winter and a sweat towel to wipe his neck were his wardrobe.

Was he to blame? How could he, an educated orphan, taken in by a crass uncle to keep cows—and thrown out because of the unfortunate go-down enterprise—how could he have more?

"Here is the modest shop of your uncle, *Babu*," Robi said, slowing down.

"It is not such a terrible shack, eh, coolie?" the passenger taunted.

"I was mistaken. It is merely a country shop—with a rustic look to it."

"Inside is a large Coca-Cola ice chest, coolie. Much much ice to make the drinks cool."

"A Coca-Cola ice chest! Then the drinks will be lovely, cold not just cool," Robi observed thoughtfully. The passenger took no notice.

Robi was resentful. This man, like all upstarts, considered only his own needs. One could rely solely on the *bhadra lok*, the gentle-folk—the Brahmins—to disburse charity. All others were money-grubbers. Nonetheless, Robi concluded, it was his duty to prick the man's callous conscience.

"Perhaps you'll bring back a few chips of ice in a clean paper, *Babu*?" he suggested.

The gross one had ears that were barricades not entrances. Robi decided to rest under the palmyra tree while his passenger satiated himself.

Someone was walking nearby, alongside the drainage ditch. It was Bahadur, the unworthy Nepali who had shamelessly used a stolen hotel bedsheet to quench a fire, and on whom afterwards, oddly, the gods had smiled. For some reason, this day, he was hiding behind dark glasses. How fat he was, like a cock before *puja* time. This was because he was fortunate enough to be cook-bearer for the personages who resided in the Lotus Bungalow.

Robi detested the Nepali, whom he saw as the incarnation of loose living: a drinker, a fighter, a friend of the woman Padmini, whose mother kept a disorderly tea shop. Nepalis were all wild mountain men, Robi believed.

Why was Bahadur walking? Every other day the rascal rode from market in his countryman Ram's ricksha because his masters were so incredibly rich they provided coins for fare. His bundle was particularly large and burdensome this day. Why then was he not riding? Then Robi noticed Bahadur's face. It was cut and swollen—and behind the dark glasses his eyes were purple. They were not eyes; they were scarred baby eggplants!

The gods were just! The Americans must have taken up sticks and beaten Bahadur at last. Though it was not Robi's habit to make conversation with the Nepali, he had to call him now. "Bahadur! Bahadur! Come and rest a minute with your friend Robi."

Bahadur headed toward him. He was equally naked, but he did not cover himself with a *dhoti*. Not Bahadur. He wore gray, red-thread-mended undershorts. What had happened to Bahadur's outer layer of western clothing? Even stripped, the Nepali moved in an arrogant strutting gait, as though he were a person of pride.

Robi was puzzled. What had *he* to be proud of? He was born and he lived. Did he regard that as an accomplishment? Donkeys and other assorted beasts had always managed it.

Carefully, Bahadur set down his bundle. He took out a *biri* and lit it. While he was tending to this, Robi scanned him closely. His face was battered, but the beating must have been some weeks past for the wounds were almost healed.

"Bahadur, what cataclysm has befallen you? Your American master, the scholar who studies words and captures them on a machine has beaten you with a stick? I gave you many warnings—even a Rockefeller is not such a fool that he would allow a servant to be a drunkard." A local Communist had once labeled all Americans "Rockefellers"; Robi enjoyed sounding knowledgeable.

Bahadur belched foul smoke like a train engine. "You are still wrong *Babu* Robibabu." It was his continual joke to shower monsoons of *babus* on Robi's afflicted head. "No master beat me. I had a fight. I fought Fat Assim the Bully—and you should see how he looks now. His face is one bashed-up pulpy mango. I punched him and smacked him around good."

"I saw Fat Assim in the marketplace this morning buying coconuts. He looked very well. His face did not resemble a mango."

Bahadur grinned shamelessly. "Assim heals fast. All that fat makes it easy for the body to mend quickly. In English that magic healing is called Ar-gy-rol. I heard a big sahib doctor telling the memsahib about it once. Ar-gy-rol." He licked his lips over the strange sounds. "But you have not heard the news, *Babu*?"

"What news?"

"I do not work for the Americans any more."

"What tale are you telling?"

"I have a much higher job now, a job proper for a Hindu. I am assistant to a Healer. That is how I know so much about medicine."

This news stunned Robi. That Fortune should twice have embraced this unworthy man was unbearable.

"If this is so, then why are you not dressed up in the fine white trousers and the shirt the Rockefellers paid for? And why are you *walking* home from market if you are a medical assistant?

"Brahmins are too nosy," Bahadur marveled. "Perhaps that is why they appear wise. They get so much information from us Kshatriyas. I do not wear my sanitary clothes to market because I wear them to give shots in."

"Shots—" Robi gasped.

"You may come sometime and peek through the window if you don't believe me. Furthermore, I did not say I was *exclusively* assistant to the Healer. I am cook-bearer as well, for the Healer is not a healthy man. Though he looks like a bull—and roars like one—his heart flutters like a bird's wings. He lets me listen to it through his silver instrument."

"Stethoscope." Robi supplied the hallowed word. "My grandfather owned one."

"The Healer takes special tablets to keep alive. This parcel contains some of the very precious cures he trusts only me to carry for him."

This was too much strange news at once. Robi sat quiet, trying to digest it all.

Bahadur spoke now with unusual gravity. "I must tell you, *Babu*, that you do not look well. Your eyes are clouded with the yellow mist of disease."

"Perhaps it is only your Bombay sunglasses and your own purple eyes that make it seem so—" Robi speculated. "Because you work for a Healer does not mean that you are one." So pleased was he with his own wit, that he restated it at once. "To work for one is not to be one."

Bahadur slid the glasses down and looked at him over the rims, pityingly. "It is lucky for you that I am carrying the very medicine that you require, right...here." He was digging in his packet and after a while he brought out an orange-colored plastic bean. "This is the magic capsule, Robibabu. The plastic will disappear inside you, and the medicine will oscillate in your blood and save you. The cure is guaranteed and the cost is one rupee only."

Robi laughed at him. "For generations my family has had medical skill. In Sylhet my grandfather knew all the secrets of the teas and berries and poultices and syrups. He was called to aid all those in the district who became ill."

"So that is how your family stole its rice money."

"Grandfather never charged for this advice. Only the costs of the medicines, if there were any, were paid by the sick.

Sometimes a grateful neighbor would give him a small offering, a fowl, or a goat, or vegetables from his garden. But my grandfather held much land. He did not need poor men's *pice*."

Bahadur snorted at that. "A Brahmin is always a beggar even though he has a hundred thousand rupees."

"I don't take notice of your ugly words, Nepali. Debased men who quote sayings against Brahmins, are merely barking pariah dogs."

Bahadur barked at him fiercely, then burst into derisive laughter.

Robi continued with dignity. "Grandfather taught father the secrets and he had begun to teach them to me—the simple ones for I was still very young—when the jackal Jinnah howled and we had to run away. Father taught me much more before he died." Robi was suffused with pride. "No, Bahadur. It is our family tradition to cure ourselves of maladies. Or die of them, as my worthy parents did—but we do not shop around in the marketplace for remedies."

Bahadur frowned. "This ailment you have is very dreadful. I know that your belly burns every night and bad dreams trouble you. Sadness sits like a boulder on your back, so heavy you can barely pull your cart. To you the road always seems uphill and steep, too steep!"

Robi, well aware of these personal torments, was greatly troubled by this speech. For an ignorant drunkard, who was neither astrologer nor pundit, Bahadur knew an astonishing number of things. How did he come to know them?

"To heal another man is to do the gods' work," he told Bahadur. "Such work must not be done for pay."

Bahadur continued to speak as though he had heard nothing. "A Brahmin much like you—only far bigger and stronger—died of this same illness last night in our courtyard. First his eyes were veiled with the yellow mist of the disease, just like yours are. Then all the water departed from his body in one soft cloud and he dried up right before my eyes. His face turned black, black as the pitch on this road.

That is why my Healer sent me early for these pills today. So we would not be unprepared when it happened again. 'If we don't have the orange pills on hand, Bahadur,' my Healer said, 'it will be plain murder when a new man suffers an attack.' Do not be stubborn, Robibabu. One rupee will bring you health."

Was it possible? Such maladies were not unknown. Every village had its share of stories and he had heard many, of possession, of horrible symptoms, and instant death....

But he did not believe Bahadur!

On the other hand, he did not aspire to have his body moisture become a cloud, while he turned black, shriveled up, and died.

"I will take this from you, Bahadur, just to sample it and see what your Healer is using. But I can give you only eight *annas*."

"Half a rupee? Impossible. I must bring the Healer his money or his drugs." No sound was spoken; there was only the heavy breathing of the two men who realized that the consummation of the deal was at hand. It was the commercial moment of truth!

"Twelve *annas*," Robi conceded unhappily. "That is my tea money."

"Very well, if that is all you have; because you are a friend—twelve *annas*."

Robi untied the money from the knot at the end of his *dhoti*. Bahadur took it happily, and handed over the strange plastic which Robi swallowed at once. "How are my eyes looking now, Bahadur?" He asked. He felt better, stronger.

"You are looking well. This medicine works miracles. The noble Indira takes one capsule every morining with her tea."

"Who told you?"

"It is common talk among Healers."

Robi was being eaten by the worm of curiosity. "Tell me, who is cooking for your old masters?"

"No one."

"How can that be?"

"They are managing with tins. Americans have a God of Tins who provides everything." He smiled boastfully. "They could not find another such as Bahadur. I cook the best goat curry in the district."

"You only say that, Nepali, because you have never tasted my cooking. I worked three whole months in the canteen of the high school, last year. The Headmaster fainted one Thursday at tea from eating twenty-three of my vegetable *samosas*."

Bahadur did not stir.

Robi knew that the Nepali had no one to recommend to the Americans because all *his* friends were toddy-drinkers and louts. Robi required this job. While Brahmins should not have to do *any* work with their hands, cooking was far better than coolie labor.

Still Bahadur was silent and he smoked.

Robi pondered. How unjust it was that power converged on such evil men, but thus it always was. Once he had asked a pundit why this was, and the wise man smiled his radiant smile and replied, "Power comes to those who need it. *We* do not need it." Often Robi had found that the pundit's wisdom was rich earth when he first received it, but useless sand when he sifted through it later.

"I will tell you what to do for the wounds around your eyes," Robi offered, proving his noble and generous heart. "Put a hot mango leaf on each one and you will see them heal. Note that I do not take any money for this advice, not one single *pie*."

Bahadur seemed uncertain. "My Healer said a paste of wheat flour was best."

An uncertain Gurkha was a glorious thing. Robi rejoiced. Then he showed his disdain for all superstition. "Bush medicine." Bahadur sat silent.

"Paste of wheat flour may be put on top of mango leaves," Robi allowed, magnanimously.

"Tonight I shall try mango leaves." Bahadur pledged.

For some minutes there was no more talk.

Never would Robi degrade himself to ask directly, but he could see no harm in restating what was already public information of critical interest. "I am a remarkable cook, Bahadur. Truly remarkable." Robi waited, hungering for an offer the way he had in childhood hungered when a friend possessed a delectable sweet.

"Is it possible that you would like the job, Robibabu?" Bahadur inquired slyly.

"Who? Me?" Robi restrained himself from leaping up and shouting: YES BAHADUR. YES! I AM A BRAHMIN. I WAS NOT MEANT TO BE A RICKSHA COOLIE! He kept his voice low and steady. "Yes, Bahadur—" He inspected his fingernails, paying great attention to all aspects—"I am a Brahmin, you know. I was never meant to be a ricksha coolie."

Again the Nepali sat quiet, hidden behind those opaque glasses. Robi could not tell his reaction because his eyes, the windows to his mind, were shuttered. Robi was sure, however, that the rascal had not spent as much time in his whole life thinking, as he did now in this conversation. He was making Robi wait for his words the way a beggar is forced to wait for parings.

They sat so long, Robi began to wonder if Bahadur had fallen into a trance. He was a *ganga* smoker so there was that morbid possibility. "Bahadur —" He nudged him with his big toe.

"I am a poor man, Robibabu. Though I have fine work with the Healer and that is a great honor, it puts very little rice in my belly."

"I understand, of course. A man who accepts a favor from another has a large debt to pay. If he is a man of honor, he will remember who helped him for the rest of his life."

Again the smoke clouds and the pose of thoughtfulness. The smoke caused Robi dizziness and made him cough.

"The sahib paid me thirty rupees per month plus clothing," Bahadur calculated. "If I take you to him, he will probably pay you the same. You will, therefore, come into enormous wealth because you get your food free. So you can easily deliver me ten rupees as my share."

"Ten rupees ? You're mad. Fat Assim spoiled your brain. Five is too many."

"Wishes never filled the bag, Robibabu."

"Six?"

"Nine."

"Six is my final offer."

"Nine."

"Bahadur, be charitable. I have not had a job in months. Some days I fear I will forget the taste of rice. Seven."

"Eight!" He stubbed out the *biri* and put the remaining bit of tobacco in his bundle. "I have no more time to talk I must help my Healer with his shots. Eight rupees is the lowest I will go and that is very kind of me. Hundreds of men would be glad to pay me ten."

"Eight." Robi consented sadly. "You are Subhas Chandra Bose, the Liberator Himself, when it comes to a War of Rupees."

Bahadur rose and, pulling his shorts up with his thumbs inside the elastic, he spat. "I am no Bengali. I am Gurkha, from a brave people. The British respected us. They formed a whole Gurkha army. I can use a *kukri* on a man the way you use a vegetable knife on a potato." He crooked his finger like the curved blade of his knife and aimed it at Robi's heart.

"When will you save the sahib's belly by introducing me?"

"Now. It is right on my way, a few meters before the turn-off to the Healer's house. It will not take long. But why are you stopping here under this tree?"

"I have a passenger, a great fat Vishnapur man who craved a sweet drink. He is resting in his uncle's shop."

"And he keeps you waiting here so long?" Bahadur was

angry. He pulled the bundles out of the ricksha and tossed his own onto the seat. "Forget the few *annas* he owes you." He climbed in. "Take me to the Lotus Bungalow at once—run!"

"Why should I be the beast to pull your cart?"

"I am getting you work."

"And what if they don't want me? Then I have lost this *babu's annas* and I have carried you for nothing."

"What if the cows stop giving milk? What if all the tanks dry up? Why, if these things happened we would drink only toddy. You are too much a woman, Robibabu, with your fears. Hurry now. To the Americans!"

Without a care for the *annas Babu* Sweet-Drinks owed him, Robi raised the vehicle, gripping the shafts firmly.

"Put wings on your feet before someone else gets the job," Bahadur urged.

Stepping off at a brisk pace, Robi had gone only a short distance when he heard the scoundrel in the cart cackling with laughter. "What amuses you?" he inquired.

"I see your passenger in front of the shop and he looks a very angry man. I know him. He is Majumdar, the Brahmin interested only in his belly. He visits my Healer for shots."

A Brahmin! Robi peered back. The Nepali was squatting on the edge of the seat, holding on with one hand and laughing so hard he was in danger of falling out. With his free hand he waved impertinently at the abandoned passenger. "Walking is good for the health, *Babu*," he shouted. "I am doing you a favor by stealing your ricksha."

"Bahadur, you should not—" Robi attempted to silence him but the Nepali became very impatient at that.

"He departed for sweet drinks and he forgot you. He used your time when you could have been earning *annas*. Did he care for you? Then why do you care for him? Let him drown in his sugar water."

Robi often thought such thoughts, but he would never shout them except at other poor men. Prosperous types always received his courtesy, because with property—and civil service jobs and uniforms—came power. Bahadur was a fool to slash openly at great banyan trees. A wise man might discreetly cut at the roots while watering the top. That made sense.

Only once more before they reached the bungalow did Bahadur speak. "Robibabu, you will keep in mind that *I* am getting this job for you. We are partners. Two rupees every Friday are due me. I will come each week, tea time, to collect."

"The fact is written in mustard oil on my skin."

"And if you tell anyone—not only the sahib or the memsahib, but any other living creature, even a chicken or a goat— about the eight rupees, I will come at night and carve you with my *kukri*."

"Do not be abusive. I am not afraid of you. But I will tell no one."

"Pull the ricksha to the side of this front yard and wait."

Bahadur jumped down and moved toward the great wooden door of the *pukka* house. Large boastful steps, Robi thought, for a small monkey in undershorts. Bahadur lifted his hand and rapped loudly, four times, like a tax collector.

Robi watched from the corner of the yard as the door opened and Bahadur disappeared. Then he turned his full attention to the gods. He asked them to grant him success and good fortune. He was sorry he had neglected them, that hunger and anger had carried him so far from the practices of his childhood. The gods were friends and protectors. It was sinful to neglect them. He made a vow that he would give offerings and prayers regularly.

The door opened. A lucky sign that the gods had heard!

"Outside is the servant that I have found for you," Bahadur was announcing in a grand manner, as though he had searched the entire province for one such.

"Robi—come!"

Robi moved forward, but, since he was not yet through the door and could not be seen, Bahadur continued his summons. "Time is precious! Come!"

A curious paradox, Robi thought. Air, light, and water are also precious—they are all of the universe, and yet all are available to the poorest man. How he would have liked to discuss this in the tea shop where such topics were often handled.

Bahadur was standing near the door in the inner yard of the house. Alongside him were the tall, fair-haired man with dark eyes and the man's yellow-haired wife. Robi had passed these curiosities many times around Khudapur. They looked to him like all other whites he had seen: eyeglasses, pale skins, ugly coarse hair; an unattractive and unblessed race. Their color was odd for human skin; it was the color of chickens under their feathers.

"Robi is a good boy—" Bahadur began, in that condescending tone again, as though he were Robi's father's eldest brother or some other person of consequence.

"I am a Sylhet Brahmin—"

The memsahib looked at Bahadur.

"Yes, he is a Brahmin," he confirmed, "but he works now as a coolie because hunger swells a Brahmin's belly too. So—he is not *so* pure. Eh, Robi? You are a *spoiled* Brahmin."

Robi's face was very hot; these words were the venom of the Himalayan cobra. But he said nothing. Bahadur was in control here. Many times in the past he had remarked on Bahadur's lowness when he saw him drunk or gambling on the roads. Now he was being repaid. "He is a hard worker and a clean person. You may depend on Robi to serve you," Bahadur finished. He wanted those eight rupees each month so he had to say good things.

The Americans scrutinized Robi. What did they see? A tall ascetic Bengali, skin the color of wheat; a serious face with lines of care already carved in the brow; bearded, for he had no *pice* for the barber and he would not shave himself. His *dhoti* was a rag, but a clean rag, and he stood straight, obviously a man with dignity.

"Have you something wrong with your back?" the sahib inquired. "You stand so stiffly, as if you're in great pain."

"No, Sahib, there is nothing wrong with him," Bahadur answered hastily. "He can work well."

The American looked at his wife and she looked at him.

Robi waited. The muscles in his neck were so tight they felt as though an iron collar had been clamped on them.

At last the sahib spoke. "We have been doing our own cooking and using tins, Bahadur. The memsahib is not happy with the *chulha* and the dung cakes, but she manages."

She made an unhappy little sound.

"Our house is quiet—" the sahib continued. "Do you drink, Robi? You must answer truthfully because we cannot keep a servant who drinks. That is why Bahadur no longer works here."

Now it was Robi's turn to look slyly at the Nepali, but he was not noticing.

"We have only a short time left here, and much work yet to do, so we cannot be troubled with household quarrels."

Before Robi could make declarations, Bahadur was speaking. "Oh, Sahib—Robi is a religious man. He doesn't drink at all. I have heard it said that he doesn't even take tea."

What was he doing? Tea was Robi's chief beverage.

"I take tea," Robi said firmly, "but I do not touch alcohol."

"Perhaps we can let Robi try working here for a month—to see if he likes us and we like him—" the memsahib suggested.

"Yes," her husband agreed. "You were very kind, Bahadur, to think of us. Thank you. Here is a gift for your trouble."

He passed the Nepali rupees. Though Robi stretched on his toes and strained his eyes, he could not see how many. Surely he would not have to hand over eight rupees this first month, for Bahadur had already received a commission.

"Sahib, I think of your well-being night and day," Bahadur declared. "It is my first duty. You will find that Robi is a fine cook-bearer."

"Memsahib will explain your duties," the sahib said, opening the door.

"Listen carefully," Bahadur cautioned. "I will visit you on Friday, Robibabu, at tea time. Cook a good sweet that day so I may test your skill." He was very bold to talk that way, but the Americans didn't seem to mind.

"Come early on Friday," Robi warned, "for I will be gone to temple if you delay."

The sahib and Bahadur departed, leaving Robi with the foreign lady who began to speak at once.

He listened carefully and though he was accustomed to the tongues of the Punjabi, the Behari, the Madrassi, and even the Chittergongian, he had never heard *such* sounds. It seemed to him that many of her words—sometimes entire sentences—were true Bengali, but it was as if her speech were broken in a mill. Nothing sounded whole. Of course, he contined to listen and to twitch his head continually to show that he agreed. One thing she said, he heard because he had been listening only for it. "No beef."

"That is good news," he informed her, saying his own words slowly, "because I never touch beef." What would he have done if she had ordered him, "Cut a cow! Cook beef!"

Then she talked on and on, oddly, about the water. Khudapur water was distasteful to her. Apparently, since she couldn't import American water in tins, she wanted the local water cooked, boiled and boiled and boiled. Robi consented, with alacrity, to send her rupees up daily in steam.

More and more she spoke; more and more he nodded politely. He was understanding better—but not all. Thirty rupees, new garments and food—that came through, for she repeated it slowly to be sure he understood.

"You will have your own room here in the house."

"I can sleep on the floor in the kitchen, Memsahib."

"Why should you? We have a room—the one Bahadur used. It's small but clean."

He followed her. She unlocked a door and they were in a white white room with one tiny barred window high up, and a few hooks in the wall. The room had furniture, a fine *charpoy* and a straw stool for sitting. How lonely it would be! In the many years of his life—he did not know exactly how many—Robi had never slept in a place without animals or other people present. What if a man had a sudden attack while sleeping all alone? He would die. It was lucky he had bought that orange medical bean from Bahadur.

Walking around the room, he stroked the walls. "In the home of my father, the walls were whitewashed too. Many times during the year the women of the house cleansed them and made them beautiful that way."

"Then you'd like the job, Robi?"

"Yes. It is the best chance of my life since malaria carried off my worthy parents and my hopes."

"Then we are very glad to have you work for us during the few months that are left."

He glanced around the room again, already rearranging the furniture so that the Nepali's time there would be erased. He would buy many bright pictures of the gods, perhaps even a mirror and some other small luxuries that would make it his home. Bahadur would have no place here, except briefly on Fridays, and that business would be conducted outdoors. He ran his fingers over the wooden frame of the rope bed. He had never raised his sleeping pallet off the ground to place it on such a cot.

"Try the light," the memsahib suggested.

He did not understand. She went to the center of the room and pulled the cord. The bulb, that indoor child of the sun, glowed. In his *own* room Robi was to have a string that brought forth a small sun whenever he wished it.

"I can read! I can study at night, after my duties are finished."

"I didn't know you could read." The memsahib was surprised. "Bahadur cannot read at all."

"Bahadur is an ignorant man, Memsahib. I am a Bengali. I read Hindi, Bengali and Sanskrit. I won honors at school until my parents died and I went to live with an uncle who kept cows. I have some training in healing, Memsahib, and I might have been a *vaid* like so many of my ancestors. Partition severed my future, Memsahib."

"Partition? That was in 1947! Surely in all those years—"

Robi bowed his head. "Family is all."

"Let's put in a larger bulb if you're going to read in here."

Americans were crazy. He had suspected it when he heard gossip of how they lived, and here was further proof. She fetched a bulb, and he climbed onto the wooden cot-frame. Just as he had finished removing the smaller bulb and was inserting the larger one, the sahib returned. Bahadur was gone from his side. Too bad. Robi had wanted him to see the glorious light. In Bahadur's place was Senbabu, the most important man on Khudapur Road, senior accountant in the local colliery. It was he who, as a Rotarian, had first welcomed the Americans into the district, and it was he who had recruited Bahadur to be their cook-bearer. Now Bahadur was playing the Big Man's Role. Senbabu would not like that. Robi's fright kept him from getting the bulb attached.

"What's going on here?" Senbabu bellowed, his eyes as angry as if he'd just caught thieves robbing his money-box.

"We have just hired Robi," the memsahib explained. "He is changing the small light bulb in his room for a larger one."

"What need has he of a large light bulb?" Senbabu inquired, all the while glaring at Robi. "Will he be embroidering mirrorwork shawls for you all night?" He stepped closer to Robi. "The sahib and the memsahib do not know our ways so you are taking advantage of them already, eh? Electricity is not free, you know; it is costly. Very costly. First that scoundrel Bahadur plays the fool with them—that drunkard—but I expect that behavior from a Nepali. *You* are a Bengali. Shame! Replace the small bulb at once."

"He didn't ask for the larger one." the memsahib said slowly. "I offered it to him so he could read at night if he wanted to."

Rough laughter came from Senbabu. "You will spoil every servant you hire. They will make a cat's paw out of you, Madam. Then they will rob you. Take this fellow—he doesn't even own a shirt. He must *sleep* at night so he can serve you faster by day, *sleep* not read. Why—where would *he* even get a book?"

"We have many Bengali books," the sahib said. "I'll lend them to him." His wife smiled a little as she looked at the angry *babu*, but she compressed her lips. Robi believed that it was the first time in the senior accountant's whole life that he had not been permitted to make the rules.

"Come, Robi." The memsahib took him to the outer door. In a very low voice, which he could not hear because of the loud talk inside, she told him some last things. He nodded many times with respect, but he was listening to Senbabu's jokes from inside. "Don't let the great scholar teach Laljit, the sweeper who comes from my house to help here. Laljit must not learn to read or my electricity bills will be boundless like yours. Oh, you Americans. You will end up doing chores while your servants play and mock you. Reading is a great luxury, not suitable for all."

The sahib's answer was soft. Robi could not hear it. He waited outside the closed door. Senbabu's voice boomed again. "Yes, the government insists on all that equality foolishness but I have always maintained that the lower castes *cannot* learn. The convolutions of a lower caste brain are different; their *biology* makes them stupid and we are wasting the seats in the schools that we keep for them—and the government is wasting all that money.

"Reading corrupts those who are not right for it. You Westerners admired our beloved Gandhi. Well—he believed this same thing about education. He practiced it with his own sons. Character was most important to him. Character, not formal education."

"Yes, we admired Gandhi," the memsahib answered with great spirit. "He would never agree with your ideas about the lower castes. And, as for his theories on education, he didn't do so well with his own sons. Harilal was a convert to Islam and—"

Such incredible boldness, for a female to speak of Gandhiji so, and to do it to Senbabu! Robi covered his ears and ran so that he would not hear the explosion.

That night Robi went to the pond and bathed as was his custom. Though the water was muddied and unclean—it was a public pond used by road people—each night he came here with his brass cup to dip the water and splash it over himself.

The water was brown. The memsahib would not enjoy it. He did not like it either, but he had no fear of it. He who had lived through riots and starvation; he who had wandered for so many years on the edge of humanity without family; he had become a stone. Does a stone rot in water?

As he sluiced himself, he remembered the fresh lovely waters of the village pond of his childhood, so clean and clear they mirrored the broad-branched mango trees above— jeweled by rosy fruit—and the earnest face of the small bather and leaf-boat sailor.

This night the young Robi was very near.

He immersed himself a hundred times to rid body and spirit of all evil, to cleanse himself so that he might be worthy of the new place in life he was to hold.

He walked to the temple and, for the first time since he had bent low to pull a ricksha, he offered prayers. Long he sat in the smoky darkness caressed by the scent of the incense and the soft sweet fragrance of the blossoms. The gracious goddess Durga, anointed and garlanded, looked out at him benignly from the inner recess.

He prayed that she would receive his petitions kindly, that he, Robi Gangulee, a poor man who had endured much would be forgiven for neglecting her. "Mother, forgive me, I shall not leave you again," he murmured. With his few *pice* he had bought flowers and, after he made his offering, he sat once again in the far corner to contemplate in peace.

He could not say how long he sat for he forgot himself in time. He drifted back into the chasm of timelessness, into those sweet days of childhood when clean and new in body and spirit, fresh from that lovely village pond, clad in pure white *dhoti* and sacred thread, he spent long hours in the prayer room at home, at bliss with the fragrance and the flowers and the great beauty of the gods of the household. That lad who so loved the gods was still strong within him; more than twenty terrible years had not vanquished him. Robi felt that night that his spirit would emerge one day to do noble deeds for the Motherland.

He slept. Peace sat upon his body soft as a golden butterfly and he was content. Whether it was the goddess who gave him rest, or whether she was assisted by Bahadur's strange orange bean, he could not say, but the hunger did not rumble in his belly nor the sweat gather on his brow. The demons of the poor man's night were elsewhere.

Alas! Would that one small demon had come to wake him at dawn. He heard neither the early gongs nor the morning prayers of the faithful so he slept on there, in the corner. No one noticed him and if it had been an ordinary day in his hapless life, not a person on earth would have cared. On a leech's body no leeches do fasten.

Rude hands grabbed at his shoulders and shook him up. It was Bahadur, red-eyed with rage as he squatted there beside him. "Robibabu, why do you sleep? The Americans are waiting for you."

Robi sat up straight and rubbed his face and eyes. Sunlight was streaming through the temple doors.

"Do you want to lose this job for us before you even start it? Do you want me to lose my place with my Healer?"

"What has happened, Bahadur? What are you saying?"

"It is after nine o'clock, the middle of the morning. At eight the American came to the Healer and he inquired, where is Robi? Where is Bahadur's friend, the reliable cook-bearer? The Healer knew nothing of this. But he is enraged that I take this time to come and fetch you.

"And so much time, Kali Ma! You couldn't sleep in the public square last night, under the ricksha like you always do. No, you had to be a *sanyasi* in the temple. I am lucky that Ram, my countryman, sleeps in the square. He guessed you could be found here. 'Robi is a *sanyasi*—' Bahadur mocked,'—and he may be found in the temple.'"

"I came to offer the gods thanks for my good fortune."

"Soon you can thank them for losing your place, and mine too. The memsahib told you that you could leave your belongings there last night. Why didn't you?"

Robi was surprised. "I did not hear her say it."

"I told you to listen carefully."

"She does not speak as we, Bahadur."

"It is true she speaks strangely. You must ask her to say her words over and over, many times, until you understand. You will learn."

"But that is improper. To tell a memsahib to say it over and over is to reprimand her."

Such fury overtook Bahadur's features that Robi edged away a little, fearing for his life.

"Are all Brahmins children? Are they all babies, crawling through life? Robi, do you want to live a man—" He choked off his words and waited till he was quieter inside. "She will repeat words as many times as you need. Nothing is improper or wrong to Americans, nothing except the drunkenness that makes a man late to cook dinner.

"You must do as I say—" He shook Robi by the shoulder. "—at once."

The priests looked forth from the small chamber to see what the commotion was about. Hastily, the two rose to leave.

"Run and tell the Americans that you did not understand the arrangement. Cook coffee for them, and white bread dipped in egg and fried in *ghee*. That will do for early tea. Run—we are partners, Robibabu, and I warn you that if there is more trouble I will fall upon you like a *goonda*."

"There will be no more trouble. The gods will help me."

"See they don't put you to sleep!"

As soon as he came to the Lotus Bungalow, he dropped his few belongings on the side of the courtyard and ran into the kitchen, ashamed to be seen arriving at that hour. The sun was already shooting hot white darts from the sky, that was how late he was.

He heard Bahadur in the office explaining to them that his excessive religion had betrayed him. "These good men who drink only tea and do not take much flesh—" Bahadur said, "they cannot always be counted on either. Robi became so occupied with praying, and his prayers were so powerful that he fell into a holy trance." Bahadur's lies were as splendid as the tales of Kalidasa. "And there he sat all night, seeing within and not outside where the sun was rising— thus he had no idea of the time."

"Do these trances occur often?" the memsahib inquired.

"It is a very rare thing, Memsahib. Only on special occasions."

Robi was an airplane in the kitchen, a jet. The *chulha* started at once and he prepared the egg-bread on that, but he longed to do another dish just to show them what a fine cook they had hired. They owned a coal stove too, a very modern one, and he attempted to light it. A flash and a clap of thunder accompanied the lighting, and his hands were fire on top. Rubbing butter on them—he had never seen so much butter in one family butterdish—he continued to pre-pare the *ghiri*, puffed rice in sweet syrup, then the coffee.

Behadur departed. Robi was relieved to see him go before some new lie was painted by his tongue on the air. Robi served the food; he was nervous because this was the first meal. The Americans were generous with their praise—and very hungry. It gave him pleasure to see how much they ate.

"But what is wrong with your hands?" the memsahib inquired.

"Some small burns.... they will heal."

The sahib insisted on examining the hands, and then on using a western cream from a tube. He had many tubes and jars in a first aid box in his office. Robi protested that he had already treated the burns with butter, but the sahib made him submit to the ointment. "This will heal it very quickly," he assured Robi.

"I come from a family of healers, Sahib," Robi said proudly. "Butter is better for burns—or castor oil."

"They are good, but this is better."

The burns healed quickly, and Robi knew it was the butter.

During that whole first week of the new job, the gods decided that Robi was a toy and they played with him. Each time he lit the coal stove, it blasted and sparked and burned him anew; each time he boiled water, hot liquid spilled on his tender skin. So immersed was he in butter—covering all his burns—that Senbabu's vegetarian dog followed him down the road one morning, eager to lick him. Robi had to run, for he dared not stone the *babu's* dog. That afternoon, when he was hastening to cut some beans, he sliced off a piece of his big toe in the vegetable chopper. His heart bounced high with joy and then low with fear because it seemed to him that he could not keep this job. The gods had found him unworthy, that was plain.

Mornings in the marketplace he struggled to get the sahib bargains. He argued and insulted and walked away angry from the sellers only to return and start all over again. His vigor was unceasing, but he was always cheated. The melons were not sweet; the eggplants were seedy; the fish smelled and the mangos were wormy. One day he spent more than an hour bargaining over a fowl only to carry it home, kill it, and find that the insides were black.

"I will return to the bazaar and give blows to that chicken-seller," he swore. The memsahib was laughing. Why wasn't she angry as any Bengali housewife would be? "No, don't go back. He probably didn't know it was a bad bird."

"Of course he knew, Memsahib. It was his business to know. I told him I was buying it for honored visitors to our country. He has no shame."

"Robi—" the memsahib smiled—"in my mother's house we have a special title for an innocent man like you to whom so many unfortunate things happen. We call such a man *shlemiel*. You are deserving of that title."

Robi was very proud. The name surely meant One-With-Whom-the-Gods-Played—in English. Some days later, when he had the courage, he asked her, "Memsahib, did you give Bahadur the title too?"

"What title?"

"Shle-miel."

"No." She laughed merrily. "That would not suit Bahadur."

He agreed. The sound of the word pleased him and he thought that one day he might carry it after his own name. He could always tell people that it was conferred by foreigners. That should count for something. Often he tasted the syllables: Robi Gangulee Shlemiel *Babu*. It had a certain ring to it.

So he survived the first days. The Americans were too kind; they seemed to be almost without interest in the vital functions of life, the cost of purchases, and the quality of food and wares. All they cared to do was read and write, talk and use their machine. Often, at first, when Robi spoke, the sahib would press the buttons and his machine would quiver and come alive; then he would ask Robi to repeat his words again and again. When he played the voice back it was very fine, like Radio Calcutta that was heard from the loud-speakers in the bazaar. Robi always tried to say his words elegantly for the machine but the sahib did not appreciate this. "I am not interested in fancy speech," he said. "I want to get the words as you say them regularly." Robi had never heard anything so foolish. On a machine a man must sound his best! After a while, the sahib was not interested in catching his words.

Each day Robi took some profit on items he bought. He was not greedy, though he thought to himself often about how many hundreds of rupees Bahadur must have stolen. But Robi was of good family, so he took just a modest tariff and he tucked it away in his room under his new *khadi dhoti* and *kurta*. A man must oil his own spinning wheel first.

The goddess Durga was his companion during the hot afternoon hours these days. He went faithfully to temple after each midday meal. The goddess had never been so lovely before. A man without rice has no caste, but now that he was eating well Robi behaved in the seemly manner of a Brahmin. On Friday he was paid. "I will need two *annas* extra for the barber," he told the sahib. "I do not wish to keep my beard anymore." He laughed. "I am not a *sadhu*."

The sahib was surprised by his request. "Why don't you just shave it off yourself?"

"The men in my family have never shaved themselves," Robi explained pleasantly. "It is not our custom."

Sahib thought about that for a while. "I shave myself," he said. "I have never in my life paid a barber to shave me."

"That is your custom." Robi stood fast.

The sahib scratched his head. "I don't understand—two *annas* is not a lot of money, but why are you asking me to pay it? I've just given you your week's salary. Why don't you pay for your own shave?"

Robi laughed at this bizarre suggestion. Of course the man was a stranger and could not be expected to know how things were properly done in this country. "It is *your* responsibility," he declared firmly. "I am working in *your* house."

"Oh—" the sahib said, and handed over two *annas*.

After preparing many extra *rasgullas*, sweetmeats made of milk and sugar syrup, Robi went off to the road barber and had himself clean shaven. Then he bathed, oiled himself, and put on his new finery. Smelling like the Tata Coconut Oil Perfumery in full production, he seated himself on the small veranda keeping with him the covered bowl of extra sweets. Thus he awaited Bahadur. In his pocket, two rupees were interred beneath a handkerchief. He hoped he would not be forced to excavate them. Hadn't the sahib already given much bakshish to Bahadur for arranging the job? That was more than sufficient. Robi was doing all the work. Why should Bahadur get so much of the money?

Ram, the ricksha-wallah, came trotting up the road. Bahadur, without the Bombay sunglasses, was seated in the vehicle.

"*Namaskar*, Bahadur."

"*Namaskar*, Robibabu. How are you?"

He hopped down and came to sit, gesturing Ram off into a far corner, out of earshot.

"I am managing well, Bahadur. The Americans are pleased with me."

Bahadur noticed his hands. "But you are cooking yourself, Robibabu! These people are not cannibals; they are Americans, not Africans. Why are you burned and buttered?"

I am a Brahmin. Work like this does not come naturally to me.

"In all the months I cooked in this house I did not wear butter once."

"You were born to serve, to be a cook-bearer." Robi moved to a new topic. "I see your eyes are healed. Hot mango leaves work well, eh?"

"Robibabu, it was as magic. The very next day the bad color went, then the swelling, and then the scars faded. You are truly gifted—a *vaid*," Bahadur exclaimed enthusiastically. "That is why I have brought Ram—" He laughed— "Ram has brought me but I have brought him. He is not healthy. He has boils on his neck that are large and hard. They pain him when he runs before the ricksha. They draw the strength from him. I told him you knew much about healing, so he came. Let me call him—Ram." Bahadur's call brought the coolie from under the tamarind tree.

At Bahadur's instructions, Ram squatted, his back to them. Three ugly eggs of pink poison lay under the sweaty skin. He had been suffering for days.

"You have earned these boils," Robi commenced. "You are merely paying for evil." This low man, this drunkard had taunted him when he was his neighbor on the pavement of the town square. Now Robi began to berate him, to insult his ancestors and speculate on his mother's chastity and sister's virginity. He lost control of his *gosha*, his fierce temper, though he knew a *vaid* must never behave in such a way.

Ram stood up, enraged. "I am going. I would smash him but I cannot hit a man on the sahib's veranda. He is not a *vaid*. He's a lunatic.!"

"*Chup*, Robi!" Bahadur ordered. "Shut up. Shame to scream so at a sick man who asks your help. And you're always talking Brahmin, Brahmin, Brahmin..."

Robi stopped. He was ashamed. He could now afford to be generous for his station was well above Ram's. "He will be all right—if the gods will it."

"What can he do, Robibabu, for the pain?" Bahadur was eager to help his friend.

"He must clear up the infection. A special secret poultice applied during the night will open the boils and they will drain. He must bathe daily using soap and he must offer prayers. He can take absolutely no meat or condiment for three weeks. If he drinks toddy—or any alcohol—" Robi predicted —"the boils will spread all over his body, his arms, his legs, his head, his behind, his penis. I have seen boils such as these many times before, hot tight pockets of poison under the skin. They are not to be trifled with. A dishonest astrologer in Sylhet once had them and he suffered for many months before he died. Not an inch of his body was without a boil; the man could not sit or lie or stand because even the soles of his feet, the very soles were puffed with poison."

Ram looked down at his feet, terrified. He was shy of speech with Robi now. "W— will you be able to get such a poultice for me?"

Robi did not reply. The major ingredient of the poultice he had in mind was fresh cow dung. Not unobtainable. "*Sri* Robi—"

How sweet to hear that tribute from the corrupt mouth! How Ram had mocked when Robi crept slowly in front of the ricksha, weary and soul-sick. Then the coolie with the boils was like a dwarf seizing at the moon to pull it down. Now the moon was firmly fixed in the heavens.

—"Will you be able to get such a poultice for me?"

"It is difficult to do, but I can fix you such a poultice." Robi acquiesced coolly. "It will be necessary to buy fresh ingredients. I do not charge you for my advice, of course, but you will have to pay for your medicine."

"How much will it cost, Robibabu?"

Robi took time to calculate. Then he told the total he had arrived at. "One rupee."

Ram whistled without sound. "One rupee!" He repeated the price. "That must be some dangerous poultice."

"It is strong," Robi conceded. "So is the poison in your body." He would say no more. He had never accepted gifts or money *before* he helped a sick person. Afterwards, sometimes, he would take a token along with the cost of the ingredients. But Ram was an old enemy and a scoundrel.

The ricksha-man understood by the silence that his credit was not good here, and he unknotted his shawl and counted out the money.

Robi received it and checked it carefully. It was correct.
"Come at the last light of day and knock on the back door
where my room is. I will have it for you. Remember the other
instructions I gave you, and don't worry. The gods help the
sick." He indicated with his hand that Ram should move
away now and wait out under the trees.

Bahadur had watched the conversation and the exchange
of money with lively interest. "Robibabu," he said in amaze-
ment, "there is a fortune in your brain."

"I might have been a great healer if Jinnah had not chased
the Gangulees. I was just beginning to learn and to read—"

"You know more than my Healer and he earns piles of
rupees."

Robi was flattered. "But I am not the same as he. I may not
take payment for my cures, or my healing powers will van-
ish. Like dust in the wind, they will blow away. That is so,
Bahadur and it has always been so. This is an inherited
ability; I have it from my father and he had it from his."

Bahadur looked thoughtful.

"I have *rasgullas* for you." Robi uncovered the bowl.

Bahadur gobbled them. "The syrup is thin, Robibabu,
but the flavor is good." He finished all the sweets. "Now you
must pay what you owe."

Robi managed to look very surprised. "The sahib gave
you rupees. I saw—"

"That was bakshish. It has nothing to do with my commission." Bahadur grinned at him. The man was shameless.

"It was payment for getting me the job. I don't think you
should be paid twice. I am doing all the work."

He did not grow angry as Robi had feared he would. The
kukri did not appear and no threatening words were spoken.
No. He just smiled at Robi the way one smiles at a child who
is pretending to be someone else.

"Robibabu, you are a smart man yet you are a big fool. I
got you this job. In one minute I could have you cast out of
this house—"

"Never. I am on time. I am steady. I do not drink."

"But you make watery *rasgullas*...I can tell them you are a thief. Or a murderer. Or I can list the diseases you have, hereditary diseases that your family has passed along for generations. They will believe me, you know."

It was true. It was as if he had them under his spell. Or rather, it was their own way of thinking that caused this enchantment—they thought well of everyone Indian. Laljit, the sweeper, regularly stole wooden matches and handfuls of salt, but when Robi reported it they never took any action. Not even a scolding was undertaken.

The landlord, the garage man, and all the merchants they dealt with directly, without Robi's intercession, were robbing them.

And Bahadur? To them he was basically a good man, even a hero, with a small flaw. He drank.

The only words critical of India that Robi had ever heard in this house were those on the first day in the argument with Senbabu about Harijans going to school—and Robi being encouraged to read.

Robi felt that the *Babu* was right about the lower castes. They lacked ability, so no matter what opportunities were offered them they would fail. He often supported this position in tea shop arguments with local Communists, by reciting the old Bengali adage: "By slitting the ears and cutting the tail, a dog is but a dog, not a horse, not an ass." However, the wisdom of permitting upper caste folk, rich or unfortunate, to become educated was, Robi knew absolutely indisputable.

"My two rupees, Robibabu—" Bahadur put forth his hand.

Reluctantly, feeling keen pain, he handed them over.

"Robibabu—" Bahadur put them away— "Work hard and we will yet be rich together." He called to the rickshawallah. "Ram—"

He climbed in, and with a grand wave like a minister-of-state, he allowed himself to be transported away.

*A*banner was stretched high across the Grand Trunk Road at the bazaar junction.

"THIS IS THE CIRCUS BHALO AND DIFFERENT FROM OTHER CIRCUSES"

As Robi walked forward, he narrowed his eyes to make out all the letters in the sunlight, and when he could read them plainly, he stopped right in the middle of that broken busy road to put them all together. So excited was he, by what he read, that he remained a statue there in the middle of the traffic till a tonga driver screamed curses at him and pushed him to one side where he struggled for a footing with a water buffalo and several bicycles.

"FOR WANT OF A SUITABLE SITE IN ASANSOL, THE CIRCUS WILL CAMP AT BURNPUR. CIRCUS BHALO AFTER GLORIOUS PRESTIGE SHOW AT CALCUTTA, BOMBAY, MADRAS AND DELHI. A FEW TERRIFYING ADVENTURES."

A circus boy in a golden turban and silver short-pants was standing beneath the glorious announcement, giving out blue handbills as fast as he could. The demand was great. Robi put shopping from his mind and went right up to him. "I will take two of your announcements, Boy. I hope they are written in both Bengali and English."

"They are, *Babu*. They are." Respectfully, he handed Robi two copies. His turban was shamefully frayed and tarnished at close view.

Robi moved to one side, away from the crowd, and read:

Human being loaded like a Gun shell and fired with thundering sound and devastating flames.

Tai Hai The Plastic Girl from Malaya.

Motorcycling inside cage of death at 60 miles per hour by daredevil girls.

Mathematical calculation by dogs.

Improvised motor car No. 420—A most hilarious comedy.

Horse riding by girls.

Jumping through flaming hoop by Royal Bengal Tiger.

Flying in the mid air by over fifteen girls of the Trapeze Champions of India.

Plus

320 Personals, 15 elephants, 24 horses, 16 tigers and lions.

Its huge tent costing over Rs. Two Lakhs can accommodate ten thousand spectators per show.

And

The expenditure on such an establishment is worked to over Rs. 4000 per day.

Our Powerful Aircraft Search Light costing over Rs. One Lakh will herald the sky at night by the throw of its beam of light to a radius of over 60 miles to indicate the arrival of CIRCUS at BURNPUR.

Nothing like this had ever come to the district before. Robi tucked the papers inside his shirt against his chest and hastened with the shopping. There was too much to buy this special day.

"Sahib, Sahib! A big event is occurring in Burnpur," he called as soon as he pulled his key from the door. "A special event, not to be missed."

The American came from the office, and read the handbill. "A circus. I've seen many circuses, Robi, when I was a child. They're mostly for children."

"Not Indian circuses. You have never seen an Indian circus. An American circus is not even a third cousin to ours!"

"Perhaps not. But I don't have a lot of time left..." The sahib smiled at him, and returned to his office.

All day Robi worked busily. Such a feast he cooked, only rajahs were accustomed to: curried goat, rice and *dal*, *lucis*, vegetable chops and *rasgullas*.

At dinner he inquired of the sahib as he served, "Have you read the whole notice of the circus? It is on two sides of the paper, you know. Such a marvel has never come to the district before."

"I read it Robi. When I was a boy, I loved the circus." He continued eating.

"But you have not been to an Indian circus," Robi said sadly.

"A circus is a circus." The sahib was too matter-of-fact. Robi bit his tongue.

In the morning, as he served breakfast, he mentioned casually who in the district had already purchased tickets for the great event. At lunch he reported the notable arrival of the elephants of the circus train. Since the sahib was reading his newspaper, he hardly took notice. At dinner, Robi carried in the rumor that he had picked up in the tea shop that the Head Lion had almost escaped and had badly mauled his brave mahout. Word was that such ferocity had not been seen before; these were, it seems, Chinese Communist lions spirited through North East frontier areas.

"Robi, have you ever been to a circus?" the memsahib asked.

"Many times. Probably more times than sahib, because my parents were landholders and could easily do such things for their children."

"Would you like to go this circus?" the sahib asked. "I am too busy to go, but I would be glad to treat you."

"No, Sahib. No," Robi protested. "I would only go to accompany you because you are a guest in my country. It is my duty to take you around."

The sahib spoke of it no more, but Robi continued to bring home the gossip. There was little else on his mind.

To go by himself would not be pleasurable; he wanted to show the stranger the glories of his country. He wanted to ride there with him in the Landrover, to be seen as his companion, to be his guide.

Friday at tea time, Bahadur arrived. Robi paid him and gave him tea.

"Robibabu, you know there is a circus in Burnpur?" Bahadur began.

"Am I blind and deaf? I was the very first to know. I was there the moment they set up the banner and gave out notices."

"Are you going?" Bahadur asked.

"I have more important things to do." Robi was brusque.

"Is the sahib going?" Bahadur wanted to know.

"I brought him a handbill, but he has more important things to do." Bahadur sipped his tea thoughtfully. "I would like to go—but I have no way to get there and back. If the sahib went, he would have room in his Landrover."

"Then I too might go along."

"I thought you had more important things to do."

"If the sahib goes, it is my duty to go with him and protect him."

"*I* could do that, Robi."

"It is *my* duty. You do not work here any more."

"Perhaps we can both go—if the sahib goes."

"He is not interested," Robi assured Bahadur. "He saw hundreds of circuses when he was a child. That was all his parents did, take him to circuses. Nothing can get him to go."

"I will try." Bahadur went inside to speak to the sahib.

To Robi, it was one of the wonders of the world that Bahadur's mind and tongue were so agile. In a few minutes, he came out to say he had arranged the outing.

"How?" Robi asked him. "How?"

"I told the sahib to bring his talking machine. People from all the local villages will be there. He will hear so many different kinds of Bengali—and that is what he wants, so he will come."

The excursion party would have been more appropriate, Robi felt, if the sahib had not taken his wife along. Circuses were mainly for children and men. But the sahib followed the unmanly pattern of having her accompany him wherever he went.

Three o'clock in the afternoon, following a lavish lunch of chicken curry, fried eggplant slices in batter, salad, and fresh pineapple, they all set out. Robi was wearing his second-best *dhoti*—a cloth of good weave—and a spotless *kurta*. Coconut oil glistened in his hair and made his shaved skin fragrant, and *ahimsa* sandals, fashioned from the leather of a cow that had died a natural death, ornamented his feet. Robi the ricksha-wallah, in his one ragged garment, was an apparition forever banished!

Bahadur looked very respectable in white pants and western, white, long-sleeved shirt. The sahib and memsahib had dressed up too, he in a green bush shirt and trousers and she in an orange dress and white shoes. Robi fixed his eyes upon her face so that they would not look upon her legs which were bare to the knee. Western women, even the respectable ones, dressed shamefully, he thought. If they knew more about Bengali life, they would behave differently. One day he would tell them much about his country and people.

The huge tent had been erected on the Market Grounds at Burnpur. Bahadur and Robi both advised the sahib to buy two First Class seats, the best seats at Rs. 2-50 for his wife and himself. The others—the sahib was paying for the Nepali, too (Bahadur had been born under a lucky star)—required cheaper seats in the grandstand. They had a long debate. The sahib insisted that they sit with him. But they would not. First Class seats were spaciously spread out on the flat ground—exactly the same level as the performance, or even lower, for the site sloped in places—so it was sometimes impossible to see anything from these comfortable seats. From the crowded seats farther back, one could see everything.

"I will buy cheap seats for all of us," the sahib suggested.

Robi was shocked. "No, Sahib. It is not fitting."

Fortunately, Senbabu came along just then with his three daughters. "Come," he called to the sahib, "you must sit with us." He looked hard at Robi and Bahadur. "You have brought these two ne'er-do-wells to the Burnpur Circus, Sahib?" He roared, his laughter so loud that people turned to see what was happening. "I am surprised that one," he pointed a ringed finger at Robi, "that one took time out from his reading to come." Again he enjoyed his own remarks, with laughter. "I suppose you will pay for their tickets too, but I hope they have not fooled you into buying First Class for them."

"No, they want to sit in the grandstand."

"Then they have not lost all sense of shame. Come. Come sit with me and I will see that you are not taken advantage of further during the show."

"Where is Mrs. Sen?" the memsahib asked. "Doesn't she like circuses?"

"I did not consult with her on the subject, Madam."

The sahib bought the appropriate tickets and they all moved off to take their seats.

With all of his imagining, Robi was still unprepared for the splendor of the spectacle. First the animals paraded round and round the tent; he counted three horses, two lions, two tigers and five elephants. They went completely around, three times.

An agile, red-haired lady, in spangled black velvet, lay down in the center, and one elephant walked over her, placing his feet carefully on either side. Halfway over, he dirtied the floor—near her, but not *on* her! The crowd was delighted by his tact. Robi called the attention of all his immediate neighbors to these details.

Marvel of marvels—the great elephants formed a ring and lifted their front legs to rest upon one another's backs. The audience clapped and stamped and cheered to the heavens.

Motorcycling inside the Cage of Death at sixty miles per hour was next attempted. The advertised daredevil girls were absent; instead, a young man in a black visored cap—who looked very much like the boy who had passed out the handbills; perhaps it was a close relative—worked at trying to get the motor started. When at last they heard it, the crowd stamped with joy. The driver went round and round the cage at least a dozen times, not too fast. But he never fell off once and he was riding on the curved sides of a cage! Robi, imagining what it would be like to pull a ricksha in that situation, yelled very loud.

Improvised Motor Car 420 was Bahadur's favorite; it was an old Ford made to look broken down. It backfired and exploded and smoked; then the entire rear section just fell off and many clowns tumbled out with umbrellas and beach balls, all wearing funny costumes and false beards and big bubble noses. Bahadur was more delighted than any child there. Robi liked this act too, but he didn't care for Bahadur's jokes. "Robibabu, look, look. There is your cousin from Sylhet." Bahadur pointed to a clown, "There is your uncle. There is your grandfather." He kept it up, once he saw that his companion was annoyed.

Throughout the afternoon, the two of them kept buying delicacies from vendors and stuffing themselves; fresh coconut slices, ground nuts, oil cakes, and soft drinks.

The tent was packed; it was a sell-out performance. Robi glanced down at the sahibs. There was much trouble in their section for many people were standing up—even standing on their seats—trying to see. "*Bosun!* is the only word the machine will hear today," he told Bahadur. Indeed, the folk still seated were chanting this order to sit down, again and again. Two of Senbabu's daughters, who had giant Sikhs standing in the row directly in front of them, were weeping, and the *babu* himself was in bellicose argument with the standees.

Trapeze Champions of India was the grand finale. People settled down again as twelve Japanese females in short red silk garments—who performed high high in the air, where they could be seen from every seat—did swings and balances and leaps leaving all spectators wondering that not one fell and was killed. From the top of the tent, with no nets!

Too soon, too soon, it was over.

Carefully, Robi rolled the blue paper program to carry it back with him. He would buy a frame and glass for it and hang it on the wall near his *charpoy*, on the head end, so that he could lie there and read it and remember this circus—and think about what might have happened to the Plastic Girl from Malaya, the Royal Bengal Tiger, the dogs who could do mathematics.

The great elephants were marched back to lead the grand parade. That same elephant, which had walked over the red-haired lady, dirtied again as the line was being formed, and the crowd roared its amusement. That seemed to be his specialty.

There was not time to see if they would form their circle and put their front feet up one last time. The crowd was beginning to move and Robi and Bahadur had to work their way through overturned seats to get to their sahibs.

A single gate was open at the rear of the tent. This was, of course, because the front entrance was sealed off to block impatient customers waiting for the next performance. For a moment Robi enjoyed the mad idea that he might hide under the stands so that he could watch the whole show again; that madness passed.

All around them, people shoved and grunted and complained, but they were good-natured, not angry. Robi quickly removed his new sandals. Bahadur did the same, then he rolled his pants up to the knees. The sahib kept his machine going as he walked, picking up words, with Robi standing close by him, guarding him. "Do not push this machine. It is valuable. You and all of your relatives could not pay for it if you break it!" Robi shouted, threatening all who came too close by waving his sandals. People could easily tell who Robi was with, and he felt very proud. Bahadur kept himself near the memsahib who was perspiring like a water jug and did not look at all well.

"Do not worry, Memsahib. You will surely get out alive," Bahadur cheered her on. "Watch where you walk now. The gate has been set right where the drains empty."

They were already in warm mud to their ankles. Senbabu, with his loud authoritative roar, blasted a deep path through the crowd, prodding people out of his way when they did not move to make room for him and his daughters. The others followed. Still it was difficult and it took some minutes, especially the last hard push through the tent opening—first they were jammed tight, then expelled violently as though being born again from their mothers' wombs.

"These people—" Senbabu exclaimed, looking down with distaste at his muddy trousers and shoes— "No organization. So backward! It is always this way." He shrugged, and with a wave of his hand he bade them good-bye as he moved toward his car, dragging the chain of his muddy daughters behind him.

The memsahib was looking down at her shoes and legs as if she did not recognize them. The mud came right up to her skirt covering all the naked skin. "A bath will take care of it, Memsahib," Robi comforted her. "It is only mud."

"You, who bathe so often and worry so much about being clean, don't mind that you were filthied?" she asked him.

"It is not pleasant, Memsahib, but is is a small price for the most glorious afternoon of my life. I told you the truth, didn't I? It was not at all like any American circus, was it?"

"No," she freely admitted.

"Better?" He looked for some enthusiasm from her.

"Different—" was all she would concede, but it was enough to make him repeat in the tea shop many times, when he was telling the story of that afternoon, that the memsahib had said there was nothing to compare with *their* circus in the whole wide world.

Robi, dreaming about the tactful elephant who walked over the red-haired lady, was trudging on his way back from market. His hands carried two sacks filled with fruit and vegetables and mutton; he preferred to walk and thus to save the ricksha fare that the memsahib provided. Suddenly, his circus fantasies were interrupted by terrible groans.

There on the side of the road was a most pitiful sight. A fat, elderly man, an exceedingly fat, elderly man, was lying on the grass, pressing his hands to his head and then to his neck, and yelling with pain. Nearby, a young boy, a servant by his look, knelt, watching. "Master," the servant begged, "what can I do to help you?" The sick man's hands flailed out at the boy.

"You rascal. To be young and healthy and to flaunt it so!"

"Master, it is not my fault."

"Oh—" groaned the sufferer piteously—"Help!" He hit the boy. "You user of all the health on the road—get out of my sight!"

Pain has surely turned him into a madman, thought Robi, approaching cautiously. Putting the groceries carefully against the tree trunk, he commanded the servant-boy, "Watch my goods and see that they are not stolen. I will try to help your master." Willingly, the terrified lad made himself guardian of the parcels.

Robi bent over the sick man, whose face was already the color of stale marigolds. He recognized that face. This was Majumdar, the passenger whom Bahadur had evicted from the ricksha. Fortunately, the invalid did not recognize Robi, clean-shaven now, neatly dressed and a completely different man.

Majumdar's breathing was shallow and irregular. "I will help you," Robi said.

"Who are you? I am a Brahmin and may only be touched and treated accordingly." The sick man lifted his head a bit, the conversation seeming to distract him from his pain.

"I too am Brahmin. I have some knowledge of medicine," Robi replied modestly. He took the victim's pulse and looked into the whites of his eyes. Then he gently pressed the neck under the ears.

"You have a blood disease."

"Yes. The healer near the bazaar treats me each week with injections, but the disease does not go away."

"How do you come to be lying here?"

"I was on my way to buy *garam masala* and certain other articles that women cannot be trusted to choose, when the spell came upon me and I fell out of the ricksha. The coolie has gone to fetch my Healer."

"Lie with your feet raised," Robi suggested. "The blood will move better." He and the boy together helped the sick man roll himself so his feet were within reach of the tree trunk. Once in place, Majumdar lay back and shut his eyes. His breathing became slightly more regular.

"If the gods will it, you will recover," Robi said, and prepared to leave.

"Do you know a medicine that will help me?"

"Try uncooked goat's liver with bile."

"This very day," the grateful man promised.

"You should eat only cooling food: sugar-cane juice, buttermilk, radishes, carrots, dasheen. And you should take absolutely —no—flesh or salt or bitter condiments."

"Oh—" the invalid groaned anew— "Absolutely no flesh? Not even at weddings or *pujas*?" He was desolate at these instructions. "None?"

Robi would have delivered a lecture to him on the Evil of Gluttony, but he was late and the Americans would be worried. He wanted to get away fast.

"Take few of the heating foods—and little flesh —" he amended.

Majumdar seemed content. He remained with his eyes closed, silent now, thus dismissing Robi without offering a gift or even an expression of gratitude.

Robi took up his bundles, nodded sympathetically to the servant boy, and resumed his walk home. He felt a combination of emotions, pride that he had helped the man and anger, great anger that Majumdar had offered no acknowledgment.

One day—Robi vowed—one day this man would require his services, and on that day—perhaps—*he* might just not be available.

In a single moment he had conjured up the poignant scene: the gross old man lying on his *charpoy*, his hands stretched forward imploringly as he cries out, "Where is Robibabu? Only Robibabu can help me! Bring Robibabu, the *vaid*" while he, Robi, resplendent in white Nehru jacket with golden epaulettes and diamond buttons, a crimson silk turban upon his head held fast by a huge sapphire stickpin, disdainfully directs his driver to turn the elephant around and ride towards Calcutta.

*A*man's destiny is as fragile as a bird's egg.

Having raised himself from the road so fast, with hard work and loyalty as his watchwords, Robi was nearly destroyed by the most innocent and commonplace of things—*dhoi*—yogurt.

He did not eat it and poison himself. Oh no. His stomach was long-accustomed to *dhoi*, having been filled with it during the years with his uncle the cowkeeper.

The difficulty began when the sahib and memsahib accepted invitations to dine out. People who have loyal servants should take their meals at home. It is not a good idea to share food at strangers' tables.

For a number of evenings, they ate away. On one of these, a Friday, Bahadur came for his rupees and when he saw no dinner on the stoves, he asked about it. Then he taunted Robi. "When I was cook-bearer here they ate at home every night. Every night!"

"Except when you were drunk, Badmash!" Robi tossed his rupees at him.

Whenever they returned from these grand meals, they mentioned the foods that they'd been fed and particularly the delicious *dhoi Babu* So-and-So or *Sri* This-and-That had served. Creamy and thick, tart and tasty, these were truly marvelous curds that had been served with the curry and rice. What every Indian toddler knew, the Americans were just learning; spoiled milk makes a great delicacy.

"Memsahib, do you know who can make excellent *dhoi*?" Robi asked, pointing to himself. "The best *dhoi* in Asansol is available under your very own roof. All that is required is fresh milk."

"We can't buy fresh milk," she reminded him. "The milk out here is straight from the cow—unpasteurized. Remember what I told you about the Frenchman and what he discovered in milk? It would make us sick."

One afternoon she had lectured him for a long time on how dangerous fresh milk was. He had not listened too closely because he knew milk to be the stream of life from the mother cow, not the bearer of death her ignorant superstitions said it was. She suffered strange fears about liquids— water too. Anyway, since she still spoke in the accents of a deaf one who could not use the language properly, he paid little attention to what she said.

—"That's why we use only powdered milk," she finished.

He hated powdered milk. It had a fetid smell and it formed into blobs and lumps that wearied the arms of the milkmaker—himself with whisk—before they disappeared.

"To make *dhoi*, Memsahib, the milk must first be boiled. I remember that you said that boiling makes it pure."

"Yes, that's so."

"Well then, tonight I will buy fresh milk right here on the road outside our front yard. Tomorrow you will feast on Robi's *dhoi*."

"On the road? Where can you buy milk on the road?"

"I will buy it from Ashoke."

"Who is Ashoke?"

"The *goala*." She required great patience; everything had to be carefully explained to her for her mind was as full of holes as a child's pockets. "Memsahib, every evening a man walks through this district leading a cow. Have you not seen him?"

"A bearded man with a stick?"

"The very one. That is Ashoke, the *goala*. Now what do you think that man is doing on the road with that cow each night?"

"Leading it home from the fields."

"Memsahib—he is selling milk."

She smiled. "You mean he walks the cow from house to house and milks it to order—a pint here, a quart there?"

"Exactly. I used to do the same in my boyhood. That is the way milk is sold in the world."

"There are other possibilities, Robi. He could milk the cow near his own house, then carry the milk about and sell it."

Such foolishness. But Robi remembered to be polite.

"Then he would need containers, Memsahib."

"Yes—" she had to concede.

"Containers are costly. Besides, if a man milks his cow out of the sight of his customer, he will add water to the milk."

"Well—he might."

"He must! This way is the wiser way. The customer observes him carefully. Tonight I will buy a *seer* of milk for one rupee. Tomorrow we will have *dhoi*."

Ashoke was from his homeland, and Robi had known him for many years. There were other *goalas* in the district but Robi enjoyed speaking with Ashoke, squatting outside at the time of the cow dust and chatting as he watched the milking.

The first *dhoi* had to be started with a bit from the market, but from then on it was pure and their very own.

"*Dhoi* is very good for the stomach," Robi reminded the Americans as he served it. They exclaimed that it was delicious, truly the best *dhoi* they ever had. Each day he made it fresh; sometimes he gave Laljit a dab with his cold leftover rice—he was a charitable man as Brahmins should be—even Bahadur had a taste on Fridays and found it consistently very fine. Ashoke and he became close friends. Until that most unauspicious day....

There are seasons in a man's calendar when nothing goes as it should, days when a sinister force seems to spoil whatever it is he touches. On the day in question the cabbage curry burned, filling the yard with its stench. The vegetable cutter slipped twice, nicking his toes and the coal iron left a burn mark on his *kurta*.

Because all these evil occurrences delayed him, he was late coming outside for the evening milking. The bucket, rinsed and covered, was out there because he always replaced it after using the milk. Ashoke, that bearded monkey, that devil, that son of a pig, had already begun the milking without him.

When he came outside, he found the bottom of the pail already well-concealed. "I will not buy this milk. It is not milk. It is water!" He declared. "All water."

"It is milk, Robi—" Ashoke laughed. "You are late tonight so I began to milk without you. But it is pure milk, I swear it."

Robi could feel the anger in his face pulling his cheeks tight. His eyes burned. "I buy two quarts of milk for the sahib each night. Two quarts of the best milk and you dare to offer me this—pig piss!" He screamed it at the *goala*.

Out came the memsahib. "What's wrong, Robi?"

"I am selling him good milk, Memsahib —" Ashoke assured her.

"It is water, Memsahib. Pond water. It will poison you,"

Now Ashoke was furious. "You want milk from a mother's breast. You want too much. This is pure milk, good milk, the best milk."

Robi bent over and smelled the milk, then he turned and spat into the dust. "I know good milk. I once kept cows. This is more than half pond water."

"Robi—" The memsahib tried to make peace. "You know this *goala* such a long time. We've been buying milk from him regularly—"

"What does that matter, Memsahib?"

"He wouldn't cheat you."

Robi laughed. "He started his milking before I came out here tonight, Memsahib. Why do you think that was? That was because he had *water* at the bottom of the bucket."

"You child of a widow—" The *goala* raised his stick.

"Please—" Memsahib put up her hand to stop him.

"A few squeezes was all I did, Memsahib. A few squeezes because it was late."

"You have many tricks," Robi accused, standing tall on the steps the way he imagined his ancestors had stood, making judgments in the village, "But I am too smart for you. I will never buy your milk again. Never."

"*You* are smart? You are a spoiled Brahmin!"

"And you are husband to a donkey!"

"At least I am not a coolie for foreigners!"

At that, Robi grabbed up the bucket and spilled the disputed milk on his opponent's face and beard, then fled to his room and bolted the door. He did not know what happened afterward for he lay on his bed weeping for a long time, hearing the murmur of the memsahib's voice then the sahib's and, louder, Ashoke's voice. Probably they paid the *goala* and sent him off. Robi would not have paid. Never. Honor was lost to the house once they dropped the coins into that corrupt hand.

A long time passed. Night came and the blast furnaces began to glow in the Bengal sky celebrated by Tagore, father of the lyric. Still Robi lay and sobbed and thought about how hard life was.

The sahib came to his door. "Robi, I would like to talk to you." He did not answer. Time passed. The memsahib came to his door. "Robi, please come out." Still he said nothing. His heart had been cut up by the *goala's* sharp words.

"Robi—" The sahib was again at the door. "We are hungry and want our meal. If you do not come out, we shall take it ourselves."

He rose at once. He did not want the memsahib in his pots. Washing his eyes at the tap, he fled into the kitchen but they followed him in.

"I do not feel like a coolie, Sahib," he said, beginning to weep again. "I eat your food. I wear your clothes. I feel as if I am your son."

"We feel that you are family too, Robi," the memsahib comforted him. "Don't mind what the *goala* said. He was angry at losing a customer."

"Memsahib, I watch your rupees carefully. I would not give them for pond water."

"We appreciate your loyalty, Robi."

"He is a thief, Memsahib, a thief who betrayed me and our country."

Robi delayed the dinner a while and ran and picked a bouquet of wildflowers for the center of the table. And while he served he mentioned to them, casually, the damage *dhoi* can sometimes do to the digestive system. Afterward, frequently, he returned to that subject. It became a favorite of his, and he offered them case histories with full details of interminable dysenteries and other related ailments he had witnessed, all the result of too much *dhoi*.

"I will never take it in the house again," he pledged. "I must take good care of you because you are strangers. It is my duty. No matter how much you beg me—from now until you leave—" he promised passionately. "I shall never serve you *dhoi* again."

"Thank you, Robi," the memsahib responded, her voice weak.

"I will make you some ginger tea, Memsahib," he offered. "All that *dhoi* from before seems to be attacking your throat. Just today I got some fresh, fresh ginger tea."

"There is much sickness about in the district," Bahadur observed, as he sat one Friday afternoon drinking tea outside Robi's kitchen.

"Yes," Robi agreed. "Sickness and evil are twins." An itinerant, wily, mirror salesman in the bazaar had cheated him that morning. After bargaining for a fine, clear mirror, he had allowed the man to wrap it in newspaper. On opening the packet at home, he found a badly tarnished glass. Great was his wrath. "If you should remove the rogues, the town would be desolate," he contined. Depressing generalities flooded his mind these days, for the Americans were preparing to leave and he would be left jobless. This prospect drowned all joy, leaving an empty deadness within him.

"You have a talent with the sick." Bahadur pursued the topic.

Robi was pleased.

"With all these diseases about, I could find you many men to cure," Bahadur speculated.

"I don't know about all ailments because I am not fully taught. You must take your sick men to your Healer."

"He is feeble these days. Only the pills keep his heart pumping. Any day now he may die." Bahadur became impatient with Robi. "I believe you already know more than he.

You know much more, Robibabu. And when a man comes to you with an ailment you cannot treat, you have only to tell him to go to the clinic!"

Robi was astonished by the fervor of the Nepali's declaration, and even more by the continued high opinion being expressed of himself.

"It is your duty to help the sick," Bahadur declared.

"But I am working *here* I have not time for other work."

Bahadur edged closer, excited. His eyes flashed as if at a holiday fete. "Robibabu, I have off from two to four and you have off from two to five daily. Let us work together during the hours from two to four. Then you will still have time for rest and prayer."

"One hour for prayers is very little time."

"The gods will understand. You will be doing their work. Look—I am giving up all my free time in the enterprise."

"But I need a place to mix medicines. I will have to buy and keep a quantity of things."

"You have a room, a fine clean place, cleaner than the clinic. Don't worry. I will help you put up shelves. I will do all."

Robi was dumbfounded by this display of selflessness. "But where can I look at the sick? They cannot come here—No, Bahadur, it is a foolish idea. I am not a *vaid.*"

Bahadur concentrated on the problem. "Wait—wait a moment. Under the pipal tree, there in the woods beside the temple. That is where you can examine the sick, in that holy place, Robibabu, outdoors but sheltered and private because the surrounding bush is very thick, like a jungle."

Robi was rather inspired by the spirituality of the suggestion. "This is very kind of you, Bahadur, to take all this trouble to help me." At first, Bahadur seemed surprised by this statement, then when he understood, he laughed merrily. "But we are partners, half for you and half for me."

At last, Robi understood. "There is no wealth in this, Bahadur. I have told you before a *vaid* does not take fees.

Doing that would spoil his special talent, and then he would not have it. He would have no more skill in healing and would become just an ordinary man. My father told me tales of such occurrences."

"He may not take fees, but he is permitted to accept gifts," Bahadur corrected.

"Only if he does not solicit them. If a sick person wishes to bestow a small present on the *vaid*, to assure his good will and perhaps his future attention, that is something else. That—and of course, people must pay for their medicines. But no fees!"

"You will leave all that part to me, Robibabu," Bahadur said confidently. I shall tell all who come to see you what a holy and good man you are. They may give their small gifts to me so that I may see that you are provided for—"

Robi frowned. This was not an idea he liked at all.

Bahadur understood his thinking. "I shall then apprise you of everything I receive. Half will be for me, and you will tell me what to do with your half. On my honor, I will hide nothing from you."

Robi's frown did not depart.

"You can trust me, I am a Gurkha. If I swear it, nothing would make me break my oath. Nothing!"

"I didn't hear any oath."

Bahadur pulled out his *kukri*. The sharp blade glistened truly in the afternoon sun. "I swear on my *kukri* that I will not cheat Robibabu," he said solemnly.

Robi had to believe him. No *vaid* collected fees. He carried in his mind the object-lessons taught by his father and grandfather.

"We will try it if you like." Bahadur's excitement was becoming his. "We will need a polished brass cup, a bucket of clean water, soap, and a clean towel under the pipal tree. A good *vaid* is a clean *vaid*. Washing must be done after each sick person is seen."

Bahadur admired his professionalism.

"I will take care of all that water and soap problem first thing tomorrow. You come just at four and wait under the tree. If I meet anyone sick tonight or tomorrow morning, I will surely send them to you. And I will be there to help."

Robi smiled and shook his head. He didn't believe that Bahadur would find a single person.

"Robibabu—" Bahadur began softly — "your tongue is very quick and dangerous. Remember when I first brought Ram to you with the boils and you nearly drove him away with your tongue-lashing? Then you would have lost a rupee."

"The rupee was for the poultice. And *he* would still have the boils."

"The poultice was of cow dung—" Bahadur smiled. "But that does not matter. You both would have lost, for you would not have been a *vaid*, helping a man which is your duty, and he would have had more pain.

"Then you quarreled with the milkman. Everyone on the road heard that one. You anger too easily. Let us agree on a signal. When I see your temper rising into your face, I shall say a secret password to stop you. When you hear the word, you must stop! That way we will bottle up your temper and it will not destroy you."

The idea intrigued Robi. "What shall the magic word be, Bahadur?"

The Nepali had to think for only a minute. Then, he smiled wickedly. "A medical word. Ar-gy-rol!"

The sahib's machine had been broken for some days and no one in all of INDIA'S RUHR could repair it. The American blamed his misfortune on the climate, but Robi privately believed that perhaps the countryside's lovely language was not meant to be carried across the great oceans. Who knows such things?

Sahib telephoned across those oceans for a new machine. Then, for more than a week he waited to hear from *Air India* that it had arrived. He was so nervous that he could not take proper food nor rest. A dozen times a day he walked to the post office to find out if there was a message—a telegram—a phone call. Americans live *this* life frantically, as if it is the only life they have.

Without his machine, the sahib could not work; he was left with much free time. Robi decided to seize this chance to tell what he had longed to say for many weeks, to speak about and explain his beloved country to this benefactor who spent most of his days listening to the clack of tongues.

"Sahib, you capture word sounds on your machine, but you do not know India. I would like to tell you what is the heart of India, and the mind, and the soul—not just the noises."

So boldly did Robi speak that evening when the memsahib had gone over to the Sens' house to study mirrorwork
embroidery. Sahib and he were alone. He wanted to teach the
visitor to peel off the surface which is only the rind—beneath
which he would discover the rich fruit of *Bharat*.

"I will be happy to listen, Robi—"

Determined to cheer the man up, by taking his mind off
the machine he was lacking, Robi breathed in deeply, stood
as tall as he was able, and began.

"I am a Brahmin you know—if that means anything any
more, Sahib. This India that you see is not my India. It is
changed, changed...."

"Still, it is a democracy and I must no longer keep prejudi-
ces about caste. I am no fanatic like the father of Senbabu
who runs to bathe and change his clothes if the mere shadow
of a low caste man crosses him. No. I am a liberal man, many
years out of the backward village.

"The only time I feel strongly is when I hear about an
intercaste marriage! Then I know it is a play by a low caste
boy to humble and contaminate a high caste family. Only
last week I heard of a *Harijan*—a Communist—who married a Brahmin girl, the only daughter of a notable Calcutta
doctor. The girl is dark-skinned and has dull thin hair—so
the only reason this rascal found her desirable, surely, was
that she was a Brahmin.

"Intercaste marriage is not common in our beloved Bengal, Sahib. Often it indicates Brahmin misbehavior. If a girl
has a father who is a drunkard, who can she wed? Again—
this unnatural mixing can be the result of poverty. I, who am
your cook-bearer, but whose father was a landowner, *I* know
this better than any man alive. If I had any sisters, who
would marry them? Their dowries would be flowers and
spiders' webs.

"I do not like what I see happening in our India today,
sahib. I hate modern behavior. I hate Bengalis who imitate
Americans, who wear fancy high pompadour haircuts and
bright colored shirts and narrow pants like bandages instead

of our soft flowing Bengali pajamas. White is the most suitable color for an Indian gentleman's garments; *khadi*, that is the cloth of the good man." He pointed to his own *dhoti*.

"I hate those Bengali youths who go about with hands in their pockets, smoking cheroots; their painted hired girls on their arms.

"I hate Anglo-Indians, unnatural people with a polluted heredity which causes great weakness. Like must marry like; that is natural law. I hate lipstick, greasy blood-red on the lips of our women. We have such beautiful cosmetics of our own, *sindoor*, the red powder with which our married ladies mark their brows; *kohl*, which makes the eyes beautiful; and henna, as well.

"You must understand, Sahib, that Bengalis have always been persecuted by their own countrymen. The others are jealous of our great culture, our art, our language—the most beautiful ever spoken by men—and our business genius. Tagore—to whom the pale blond people in the cold distant country gave a great prize; it was honor and money both—was a typical Bengali. Typical!

"The national government has been most unfair to us over the years, taking business away, raising taxes, trying to lessen the power of Calcutta. We are fighting back. Ah yes, we are. The Congress Party of today is not the party of Nehru and Gandhi. It is another Congress, a party of insincere people. I do not say all are insincere, but many, many. Too many. The central government is like an old sewing machine. Something breaks. It is fixed. Then something else in some other place breaks. That is fixed. So it goes, on and on.

"Our India is being damaged by corrupt movies everywhere. Naked women's legs and evil stories entertain our people and vice is rising and spreading like a river in a great storm. Soon it will overflow its banks and drown us all. Once I too went to a movie, when I was very young and foolish and had bad companions who tempted me. It made me ill with a pounding in my head so that I had to run away from the movie house and the evil in it.

"Libertines speak now of free choice in marriage—such as you have in your far-away country, Sahib—for Indians it will never be right. For us, marriage is very serious; parents and matchmakers must search carefully for the proper mates; horoscopes must be in accord and dowries require systematic arrangement. How can a young boy or a young girl know enough to choose a life partner? Life is long and hard.

"For myself, I shall never marry. I want only to live to do honor to the gods and to my parents and to my grandfather's name, to heal the sick whenever I am able and to offer tribute in the temple to—"

Robi had much more to say but he was interrupted by a terrible knocking. It was only Postmaster Mohan, exercising his authority at their front door. His was the daily newspaper that Robi read aloud each night in the tea shop; Mohan was a civil servant and therefore could afford newspapers. He was a fairly important person on Khudapur Road, who did not often deliver messages himself. In fact, he had seventeen children to do such errands for him. But this was the message for which the sahib was so anxiously waiting. Mohan could do no less than carry it himself.

The sahib gave him bakshish and dismissed him. Then the sahib read the words on the yellow paper; with great joy, he spoke. "Robi—my new tape recorder is in Delhi!" He paused thoughtfully. "It is odd that they didn't ship it on to Calcutta where it would be easy for me to pick it up. Oh well—perhaps there are formalities, licenses.... Let me see; this is Friday. If we set out early tomorrow morning, we would be in Delhi on Sunday when all the offices are closed. Therefore, we will travel on Sunday so that we can get there in time for business hours on Monday. We will stay through Tuesday in case there are any complications or delays—and start back on Wednesday morning.

"We, Sahib? Who we?"

"You and I, Robi. Memsahib wouldn't care for such a long train ride just to get a machine. She will stay with the Sens while we're gone. Would you like to come with me and help me?"

Robi come with him? Robi who had never been as far as Calcutta? He would have kissed the sahib's feet just then, but the sahib never allowed that.

"I must run to the railway station and get on line for tickets at once, Sahib. It is not always easy. I hope there will be places on the train for us."

The American gave Robi money and instructed him to buy two first class tickets.

"First class tickets for Sunday," Robi told Bahadur, "and may my tongue be severed at the roots if I am lying."

He had, first of all, detoured on the way to the ticket office because he couldn't wait to see the Nepali's face when he heard the news. "Delhi!" Bahadur had repeated, "Delhi!" and into his eyes crept envy and great remorse at what might have been his incredible opportunity and was lost.

Robi was too happy to lecture him on the Evil of Drunkenness, which was fortunate because it might have been a dangerous thing to do just then.

The second reason for Robi's detour was to suggest that they postpone their medical project under the pipal tree for several days until his return.

"No," Bahadur decided. "Let us try tomorrow to see how it works. Then we will give it a rest while you are gone."

*A*ll through history, medical men, no matter how complex their training, have relied primarily upon the healing power of nature. Robi was just one more practitioner in that noble tradition.

Next afternoon as soon as he had finished his chores for the Americans, he bathed rapidly then oiled himself. After donning a clean *dhoti* and *kurta*, he hastened down the road toward the pipal tree. There he planned to remain, to rest in the soft green shade saying *mantras* and meditating. If Bahadur had been at all successful that morning, in his advertisements in the bazaar and the tea and toddy shops, there might be a few sick folk coming to the tree.

Robi doubted greatly that anyone would appear. Therefore, this pessimist-in-good-standing was astonished to see five—his tongue actually counted, confirming for his unbelieving eyes—FIVE PEOPLE, three squatting and two standing, all in a sort of queue that Bahadur was supervising.

Robi reduced his pace to one befitting a dignitary. To the onlookers he appeared suddenly to be moving backwards rather than advancing, but this illusion was eventually dispelled when he arrived under the tree.

"First—" He got down to business at once.

The first patient was an old farmer, a tall, dark-skinned, bewildered man. Robi took his pulse without saying a word to him.

"I have never been ill one day since I had malaria as a small child," the patient volunteered. He was blinking and twitching about with nervousness. "Suddenly, I have pains, terrible pains and there is swelling."

Robi realized at once that his ailment must be a delicate one so he escorted the man back into the deep bush in the center of which Bahadur had used his cutlass to clear out a circular area almost five feet in diameter. The examination room! Robi inspected the swellings which were in the groin; they were miniscule bumps, unbearably tender to the touch.

"This is a very painful ailment," he sympathized, "but it is not serious. You must bathe, and offer prayers and rest. There will be a medication here for you tomorrow—to rub in gently—and I will say a *mantra* for you. With the help of the gods you will be cured in three days." Honey and lime paste, Robi knew, would relieve this man's ills. He remained in the bush a little while, afterward, to meditate.

How grateful the old farmer had been. Robi worried that the costs of the medication were not mentioned, but his mind was relieved when he saw Bahadur take the swollen-glands man to the side and speak very earnestly with him. Indeed they seemed to be disputing some controversial topic.

But Robi could not use his precious time to inquire further.

Conspicuously, he rolled up his sleeves to wash his hands.

"Bahadur—" he called. "Bring the water."

Bahadur filled the brass cup from the bucket he had provided.

"Pour—" Robi commanded, bending forward a little, his feet well apart. Once the hands were wet, Robi kept them well in front and lathered them with soap. Then he studied them carefully to see that every bit of skin was covered.

"Wash—" he ordered. Again Bahadur fill the cup and poured.

"Rinse—" Once again Bahadur filled the cup and poured water carefully so that the soap was washed off. He was about to put down the cup when Robi spoke once more.

"Towel—" He dried himself, then carefully unrolled his sleeves.

"Next—" Robi was ready.

Next was a thin young woman in a shabby green *sari*. Her pulse was very slow; she had fallen asleep while waiting her turn and was groggy even now, during the examination. "I don't know what to do with her," her hawk of a mother-in-law complained. "All the time she is tired and she wants to sleep." The mother-in-law was wearing gold jewelry; she obviously had some wealth.

Exhaustion and overwork were Robi's diagnoses but he did not reveal them to the predatory woman who stood before him, guarding her captive so zealously. "She will recover," he said. "She requires nourishment: almonds, pistachios, and quantities of milk. Of course, no meat." It was unlikely, Robi thought, that this girl ever tasted meat anyway. She was to be allowed to sit in the sunshine mornings, before the sky heated up. And she was, under no circumstances, to be overworked for at least a month.

"A month!" The mother-in-law was appalled.

"God helps the sick." He cheered up the older woman. "Then she will be all recovered and able to do the work of three." It was exactly the right thing to say. Never once did he look into the patient's face, so that the mother-in-law was pleased with his properly respectful demeanor as well as his prognosis. "I shall say a *mantra* for her," he promised, and turned away to the tree for silent reflection. The mother-in-law was delighted with him. Robi was a professional, born to what he was doing.

Though he had prescribed no medicine in this case, he noticed with interest that Bahadur had acquired a large brown fowl as the ladies departed. Bahadur too was a professional, born to what he was doing.

They repeated the washing ceremony, step by step. Bahadur filled and poured and Robi soaped and scrubbed and rinsed.

"Next—"

Here was a powerful man, a laborer by his appearance. He had remained standing while he waited, leaning on a strong staff. He limped toward Robi, obviously in great pain. Again, Robi first placed his fingers on the man's wrist and concentrated.

"A truck ran over my foot," the man lamented. "I was working on the road and a truck came from behind just as I stepped out, and it mashed my foot. Just then the Nepali came by and he told me not to fear, there was a *vaid* who could help me. That foot feels like fire inside."

Robi knelt and gently felt the foot all over. Nothing was broken, but it was swollen and discolored. "I will help you but you cannot work any more today or tomorrow—and maybe not the next day either—you will have to see how you feel. You must go home to rest now. Tomorrow you will send some relation to get a powder from me. You must mix the powder in a cup with a little warm water—warmth is very important—then dip a cloth in the mixture and wrap your foot in it. Keep the warm wetness on it until the foot feels all recovered. I will say a *mantra* for you." He turned away from the man, confident that the combination of saffron and limestone would work well.

"Bahadur—" he called. "Bring the water."

Now the single person left under the tree was the red-faced elderly water buffalo of a man who also had remained standing all through his time there. Probably his size made it impossible for him to squat, and there were only two positions for him: vertical and horizontal. He was Majumdar! Robi had recognized him at once even though he'd last seen him in a horizontal position.

As he washed himself most thoroughly, Robi speculated: How had Bahadur ever directed that dignitary, that propertied glutton, that veritable zamindar, here?

Bahadur, unraveller of life's intricate mysteries, proceeded to introduce the gentleman.

"Doctorbabu—"

Robi thrilled instantly to the title.

"This is Majumdarji from the village of Vishnapur. He told me a remarkable tale of being saved by a holy *vaid* one morning on the road to market. I recognized at once who he was speaking about because there is only one such in the whole district.

"After the Healer ordered his shot today, and I provided it, I whispered to him that I knew you and I told him further of your remarkable skill and learning. I am a loyal assistant to my Healer and I would never send a client elsewhere, but when I see this good and upright man, headman of Vishnapur, known for his generosity and kindness, suffering, I cannot bear it."

Bahadur wiped away a tear.

Majumdar gazed at the Nepali as one might look on a beloved youngest son. The tableau remained so, for Robi had no idea what to say, until Bahadur spoke once more. "Can you give him some further advice?" he implored. "Save him!"

Robi reached for the old man's hand and carefully using his three fingers properly, took his pulse. "You will be all right," he announced after a bit.

The worry became slightly less carved on the zamindar's face. "What must I do?"

Now that he was upright, it was easy to see that he was overweight about twenty kilos.

"You remember that day on the road I told you to take only cooling foods? And give up *flesh*." Robi reminded him sternly. "The worst thing in the world for you is heavily seasoned meat. Mutton curry! Goat curry ! Lamb curry!" He began to grow very angry with this Majumdar whose passion for meats was akin to a dog's. "You are poisoning yourself with the deadly—"

"Ar-gy-rol, Doctorbabu—" Bahadur sang out. "Ar-gy-rol."

He didn't know why Bahadur would not let him speak bluntly to this foolish man, but since for all the years of his life his temper and his sharp tongue had damaged the meager possibilities open to him, he now obeyed the signal. While it was plainly his duty to scream at Majumdar to avoid salt and flesh and to eat only vegetables—such an important and willful man would not listen to quiet advice—Robi remained silent.

The small ferocity he had revealed, before Bahadur quieted him, had impressed the villager. He did not ask Robi to relent on the rules. Instead, he said, "Do you have a new medicine for me? Doctorbabu, the goat's liver with bile helped me so much."

Medicine was far easier for him to manage than dieting.

"Yes. Tomorrow you must send your servant-boy here— by the way, that boy needs milk if he is to work well for you; I saw it in his eye-color—send him and my assistant shall have for you the classic formula from the *Veda* for your ailment."

"May one ask what the ingredients for the potion are?"

Robi looked at him sternly. "One may not ask a *vaid* such a question." He could imagine the old man's reaction if he told him he was going to get pigeon droppings mixed with honey in the proper proportions.

"But you told me about the goat's liver with bile, that day on the road."

"I wished to help you and I did not think I would ever see you again, so I revealed my secret. But I have never done it before, nor will I ever do it in the future."

The old man was pleased. "You will recover," Robi predicted. "The gods help the sick."

Still Majumdar remained waiting. As he was gluttonous with food, so was he with other men's time. Robi raised his palms together to indicate that the interview was over; then he turned away and sat in silence. Majumdar watched for some minutes and was terribly impressed by the holiness of the situation: the pipal tree and under it the ascetic *vaid*.

Then Bahadur walked with him a little way down the road, detailing the costliness of the preparation that was to be mixed for him.

"Why did you not let me scream at Majumdar to avoid salt and flesh and eat only the plainest of vegetables?" Robi asked, when they were alone. "He will not listen to *timid* advice. It was my duty—"

"Robibabu, it is your duty to our partnership to take care of him and tell him nothing. The more he stuffs himself, the better for us."

"Bahadur—I am a religious man, a moral man. I do not want to commit acts that will damage me—I have many lives left to live."

Bahadur saw that he had to placate him. "Robibabu, how good-hearted and foolish you are. Do you know nothing of men? For sixty years Majumdar has been stuffing himself while all around him village children starved. For his last daughter's wedding he gave a feast that fed five hundred rich kinsmen who were already far too fat. They came from Uttar Pradesh and Bihar, decorated with gold and glittering jewels; from where didn't they come?

"I know because I went to wait in the outer courtyard for leftovers. What heavenly food, everything cooked in *ghee*. No peanut oil for Majumdar. Oh, they feasted like gods at that wedding and they live like gods in the village, the rich ones. They don't notice what's happening around them and they don't care.

"What effect will your angry words have on Majumdar? They will only be pebbles that hit him in the face and anger him. Give him medicine that he may feel better, and I will collect his tokens to you. That is your duty—and mine."

He was, of course, right. There is no use pounding an ass to make him a horse.

On Sunday, in the freshness of the early morning, amidst a thousand admonitions from the memsahib that they be careful not to drink any water—the lady was eccentric on this subject—the sahib and Robi boarded the car behind the great coal-burning engine at Asansol station. A whole small room containing special shelves to place their bedrolls on at night, had been rented.

This room on the train was about the size of an adobe house of an average poor villager; one could stroll about in it. That is, when one could stand. Robi was wobbly, but in a few seconds he had learned to balance himself.

"You learn quickly," the sahib said.

"So my schoolmasters always noted."

During the cool hours of the day they rolled through the sweet green fields of Bengal, Robi waving both hands delightedly at all the villagers and children they passed. Many waved back.

Lunch was carried in from a station kitchen, curry and rice, moderate portions, and fruit in custard. The curried chicken was well-flavored but greasy. As they ate between stations, Robi observed, "Not as good as I cook," and the sahib agreed. "There is much fine black dust in this food,"

Robi noted critically. "Still it is a wonderful thing to have a cooked lunch served on a moving train. India is so beautiful as it passes by out the windows; with such great trains as this she is surely the number one country in the whole world. What other place is like India!" he exclaimed.

After eating, and marveling at the system whereby the dirty dishes were removed by a waiter at the next station, Robi went for a walk in the corridor. He was softly singing to himself, "Mother, I shall weave a chain of pearls for thy neck with my tears of sorrow—" when he was interrupted by a small dapper gentleman about fifty, wearing a navy-blue blazer with an emblem on the pocket. This notable, who had few hairs on his head but had distributed them evenly over the shining surface, waved a clothbound book at Robi jovially. It was the *Gitanjali*.

"You are singing a very great favorite of mine, a very great favorite." He introduced himself, R.P. Mukerjee from Calcutta, a civil servant and a Tagore devotee.

Robi was flattered by this man's attention; he knew that his being on the train made Mukerjee think him a worthy companion. In Asansol, a Mukerjee would not discuss literature with a Robi.

Once this scholarly man extracted from Robi that he was accompanying an American scholar to Delhi, he hastened along without delay to make the acquaintance of the foreign scholar. Then he chose to sit with him and talk of Tagore— and he talked and talked and talked. He knew quantities: how the name Tagore was originally Thakur from the family's official duties for the Moslem rulers of the seventeenth century; how Tagore's father on a journey by palanquin stopped under a lovely tree and found such peace and tranquility in the shade as he rested and contemplated the great deserted plain, that he bought the place and named it Shantiniketan which means abode of peace; how the poet's parents were so conservative they kept the boy away from bad company; how Rabindranath took to writing poetry as a remedy for loneliness; how fortunate for the world he was lonely since that is the only way art thrives; how he received eight thousand pounds as his Nobel Prize and put the money all into the Shantiniketan School; how he was knighted in 1915; how he resigned his knighthood in 1919 because of the shameful methods the British were using to quell disturbances in the Punjab. How much gossip he knew!

Thus the small carp flits about.

The sahib said very little. Mostly, he looked sleepy and a half dozen times he politely covered yawns. But R.P. Mukerjee took no notice. He himself, though a small rather frail man, had vast energies. He took his meal with them that evening and left them only to sleep.

"What would Bengalis talk about, Robi," the sahib wondered, "if they did not have Tagore?"

It was a sobering thought.

In the morning, Robi had locked the door, but R.P. Mukerjee came and knocked insistently until he opened it. "The locks are always broken in the trains," Mukerjee complained. "I will write a letter to *The Statesman* about it, at once."

He talked on through the hot stubbly fields of Uttar Pradesh. "I must recite my favorite verse for you. It is of course, from *Gitanjali*. He rose, placed his feet wide apart and commenced:

> Where the mind is without fear and the head is
> held high;
> Where knowledge is free;
> Where the world has not been broken up into
> fragments by narrow domestic walls;
> Where words come out from the depth of truth;
> Where tireless striving stretches its arms towards
> perfection;
> Where the clear stream of reason has not lost its
> way into the dreary desert sand of dead habit;
> Where the mind is led forward by thee into
> ever-widening thought and action—
> Into that heaven of freedom, my Father, let my
> country awake.

"Very fine," the sahib said. "Now we are approaching Delhi. We have to prepare to leave the tr—"

"Yes," agreed R.P. Mukerjee. "We are approaching the place where all tracks converge. I must note that—it is a good line. I am also a poet," he confessed, giggling. He moved a step towards the door. Perhaps the sahib thought he was going; Robi knew better.

"You are fortunate to have such a fine servant—" he began his valedictory. "I trust that your business in Delhi will be speedily concluded and then you will return to my lovely state. Of course, Asansol—" He made a wry face. — "Still . . ." He braced his shoulder against the bed shelf and wrapped his arms around himself. "I should like to offer a few words of advice to you about Bengalis, which will enable you to better understand us. We are quite snobbish, but that is only because we are an ancient people. It is nothing personal, merely the expression of our Bengali superiority.

"You have heard that we are orthodox Hindus and therefore you must never offer us alcoholic beverages in your home."

"Yes, I know. I've been here for many months," the sahib reassured him.

"Many Bengali Brahmins eat meat so you need not hesitate to offer goat or mutton or lamb. I myself fancy lamb. We are also great fish eaters; the *rui* fish is—"

"I know," the sahib said. "I have lived here a long time."

"For years now, Europeans have been interested in our superior culture, so we are quite accustomed to being studied. Indeed, the more sophisticated Calcutta families often count a resident linguist like yourself—or an archeologist or anthropologist—as part of their households. You have much to learn from us, much, much, much."

Sahib nodded. "Now you must excuse us. We have to pack up—"

"Since you are so interested in Tagore, I am sure you would like to take a subscription to our little Tagore Society journal. In it are many learned essays about the poet."

The sahib looked reluctant.

"Scholars must support one another. I can tell you all about the last issue which was profound. The first article—"

"How much?" the sahib reached into his pocket.

"Ten rupees."

The sahib handed the money over. "I would like a receipt—for my accounts."

R.P. Mukerjee shook his head, "In India it is not our custom to give receipts in literary matters." He smiled in a most friendly way. "I am returning on the train tonight. Is there a chance that I can have the pleasure of your splendid company on the way home?"

"Oh no, our business will take several days," the sahib said. "Maybe weeks."

"Maybe months—" Robi added.

"Too bad. It has been an incredible pleasure for me—" R.P. Mukerjee was almost weeping.

"Don't you think you should take my address—for the journal?" the sahib asked.

"Address? Oh yes, yes, of course." It turned out that he did not have a blank bit of paper on him, so the sahib provided it.

The train lurched and stopped. R.P. Mukerjee went, at last.

"Robi—" the sahib said in a low voice. "Never, never, never speak to strangers on a train. Never!"

"I did not know, Sahib—"

"Never!" he said, and began to laugh, and the two of them continued to laugh together as they made their way off the train.

Old Delhi Station was a commotion; much larger than Robi had ever seen, it was crowded with people, some sitting on the platforms with their produce, bundles, bedding, brass pots of food and live fowl; all in the way. Others ran about madly, knocking against people in their efforts to get somewhere. Vendors were selling ice cream, newspapers, curried foods, pastries, tea. All over, one could see holy men, shoeshine boys, and beggars. There were dozens of porters in red jackets and they all were shouting angrily. Robi fought them off as they tried to grab the sahib's luggage. City thieves; if they got their hands on the things, they would disappear forever.

The sahib had decided to stay where an American friend of his had once stayed, the Broadway Hotel. Robi secured a taxi. The driver argued that they should go to *New* Delhi which the British had built in 1931, he said, and therefore it was clean and modern. It had hotels with chemical swimming pools and English dining rooms that served beef. But the sahib would not change his plans.

So their car moved with difficulty through narrow streets jammed with bicycles, scooters, taxis, horse-carriages, pedestrians, dogs, buffalo carts, and children. Refreshment stalls crowded the sidewalks; fruits, nuts, fried savories—and *pan* was everywhere available. Whenever there was a traffic tie-up, the taxi was instantly surrounded by beggars holding forth their cups and bowls and hands. Robi had to scream at them and chase their arms from the windows. There is not enough wealth in the whole world for the beggars of Delhi.

At the hotel, again it was a struggle. Robi was determined to carry in the sahib's luggage. Even so, too many people served them. There was a doorman, a desk-clerk, and a lift-operator, all of whom came right into the room with them and did not depart until the sahib had tipped them— though Robi made many loud general observations about the greediness of the urban human species.

No sooner was that crowd gone, than a room bearer appeared. He filled their Thermos nicely with ice water. Then he fell to his knees and began to weep as he told the sahib how his small son was ill and required medicine.

"Tell me what is wrong with the boy, for I am a *vaid*—" Robi tried to interrupt the torrent of words, but the man did not heed him. His baby would die, it seemed, if he did not have five rupees at once. Would the sahib advance him the money? He would serve them loyally during their entire stay, doing all the chores they demanded of him and much more. Robi began to scold him and wanted to give him blows for troubling the sahib who was so hot and tired from his trip, but the sahib silenced him and gave the man the money.

They never saw him again. He was a *dacoit.*

How he got into the hotel with the ice water, no one knew, and when Robi told the story to the true room bearer, he was astonished, then furious. "Those were my rupees," he kept muttering again and again under his breath. "My rupees, my rupees." So it is in the very large cities; danger and dishonesty lurk everywhere.

The sahib bathed. Then Robi bathed and they set out right away for the Customs House. Robi carried his posses-sions in a thick cloth; he trusted no one, but the sahib left his suitcase in the room. It was a hot morning, cloudy and gray, the day of the calendar that is the holiday *Raksha Bandhan*, when sisters tie elegant costume bracelets on their brothers' wrists and in return the brothers give their sisters money, gifts, and renewed promises of protection. Their taxi driver had a butterfly bracelet of gauze and a tinsel-flower bracelet. "I gave my sister a new *sari*," he confided. "We are a good family, only poor." He noted Robi's bare wrists. "No sisters, eh?"

"No family at all," Robi told him, and the man sighed and looked very sad.

Their trip brought them through the slums—the *bustees*—never-ending stretches of filthy shacks without water, crowded all like crazy boxes on top of each other. Robi, poor all his life, was frightened to see how terrible it could be in the city where trees and grass and even a blast-furnace sky is denied a man.

The tax building was vast, like a castle, with hallways going every which way. Sahib, carefully carrying his papers in his thin briefcase, stepped briskly along to Room 134, Robi right behind him. It was ten o'clock; they were in very good time.

They took seats on the bench provided for waiting, and they waited for three hours. During that time the skies darkened and rain fell in floods outside.

This was a huge bare office furnished only with several clumsy tables, some wooden chairs, and about four almost-dead ceiling fans. Hundreds, thousands, probably millions of graying broken folders and splayed folios crammed with ragged papers were spilling over everywhere.

A single tax official was king here. A plump man with a dark skin and a bristly moustache copied from the British, he had cheeks that worked like bellows. His manner was loud and brusque. Whenever he spoke, it was to shout—at the clerks or the khaki-clad peons who carried the piles of paper in and then carried them out again. This official saved his choicest growls for foreigners.

There were two Afghans waiting on the bench behind; Robi recognized their loose clothing and their blue and white turbans of toweling cloth. They sat quietly; then one tiptoed forward to ask a question, his passport held in his hand. The official was leisurely turning papers in a folder. He continued to do this with the greatest indifference.

The Afghan paused, then he repeated his question, bending low almost double, in his effort to get close to the official's hearing range.

There was no response.

After several minutes in that position, the Afghan turned to retreat. Just then, the bureaucrat looked up. Angrily, he demanded, "Why are you standing up here?"

The Afghan began to stutter. "I-I-I desire to know, S-S-Sahib, if I am in the r-r-right office."

"Is this your turn on the queue?"

"No. I-I merely require information. Is th-th-this the right room?"

"If it is not your turn on the queue then you have no right to speak. You just march right back to the bench and wait. This is democratic India where each man is taken in turn. Just because you are a foreigner, do you think it is your privilege to go out of turn? Foreigners no longer have those prerogatives in India. We are a democracy here now!" He sneezed as if to emphasize the point. "Democracy means you wait on line!"

The Afghan lifted a hand to stop him, to explain.

"Not a word," the official shouted at him. "Do not answer out of turn. Go back to your seat and wait."

Robi feared that things would not go well for the sahib; this dignitary was not fond of foreigners.

"Come—" The sahib was summoned. He motioned for Robi to move forward with him.

"We are together," the sahib explained, and the official—after looking Robi over with scorn—snapped his fingers. A chair was provided for Robi, a most remarkable piece of furniture with four legs of different lengths and a cane seat torn in the center. Robi did his best to balance in it without falling over or through.

Now that he had them seated directly in front of him, the big man could go back to his reading. He arranged his face in a scowl, lower lip thrust forward as a pocket into which the stiff moustache was tucked. He was a bureaucratic tiger!

"You are planning to sell this machine, Professor—" he accused. He had a bad sniffle, a rainy season head cold, Robi diagnosed, probably of many weeks' duration.

"No, it is for my own personal use."

"But you brought in another machine when you came!"

"Yes. That one is broken."

"Show it to me."

"I didn't bring it. It's useless."

Disbelief lighted the inquisitor's face. "One is useless and the other is new. You will sell the new one before leaving India, isn't that your scheme?" His elbows were on the desk, his eyes narrowed, his body rigid, upright, barely allowing breaths; he was a keen, unimpeachable civil servant, a detective who trusted no one!

"I am not permitted to sell it. It belongs to my research project. The money for it has come from the United States government."

"You will have to get letters from the American Embassy, and testimonials from many scholars and big men for me to believe such a tale. You really do not expect the government simply to take your word. We would be cheated out of hundreds of thousands of rupees each year if we just took men's words."

The tax official grabbed up a handful of documents and began to read, emitting harsh sounds, each somewhere between a cough and a sniffle and all managing to convey disbelief. His breathing was hard.

"Sir," Robi ventured, quivering as he spoke, "forgive me, but I have in my bundle some fresh ginger tea I acquired yesterday and brought along on this trip in case of illness. I should like to present it to you. There is no cold cure like ginger tea from Bengal—"

The man's face lit up like the heavens when all the constellations shine forth. "Ginger tea! You are Bengali!" He raised his hands, pressing his palms together. *"Namaskar.* I shall be glad to have some tea from home."

While Robi fumbled in his cloth package, he pressed his advantage. "Sahib speaks Bengali, you know. He is doing great work there and I am assisting him."

"You speak Bengali, Sahib?" The tiger was hypnotized.

"Ha. Yes."

"Where did you learn?"

"In Chicago."

A look of exquisite joy transformed the official's face. "In Chicago, the United States of America, they speak Bengali?"

"At the university, they teach it. My wife also speaks Bengali. And my assistant, here—" he indicated Robi, who tried to sit up tall and proud but the legs of the chair wobbled—"He is a Bengali scholar."

The patriot turned to Robi in his bewilderment. "No Europeans ever bother to learn our language, Brother. Hindi, Hindi, Hindi, that is what they study."

"These are not ordinary Europeans. They do not ever take beef," Robi testified. "Here is the tea. Let me also give you a fresh twig from the *bel* tree to wear on your person." He handed over his gifts.

It only took the bureaucrat one minute. Then his tongue began to race and his eyes to dance with joy and power. "Of course you must have your machine, Sahib. Such stupidity to keep your scientific equipment from you. Please forgive us. We are still a young country and sometimes the bureaucracy inconveniences—" He set to work assembling and collating and filling out and stapling. Many copies of various documents had to be signed by the sahib.

At last the tax collector rose and clapped his hands briskly. A peon stepped forward and was handed the precious sheaf of papers, large and heavy—in this world, the more papers there are about you, the more important you are. "Take the sahib and his assistant downstairs and see that he is given his scientific machine. At once!"

He came round the desk to them, and this time his voice was as sweet as the *bulbul* of his home. "I am glad to have assisted you because you are doing noble work in the land of my fathers." Lowering his voice, for it was a central government office, he said, "We are a great people that have been cut apart. We have a magnificent culture, an ancient noble culture. One day Bengal will rise again to lead all of India! And probably the world! Surely you have heard of our Tagore, Professor—"

The American, an apprehensive look on his face, quickly clapped his palms together in polite farewell. "Of course," he said. *"Namaskar."*

The official responded courteously in the same manner and stood beaming after them as they followed the peon out.

"Robi, you are a great *vaid*, a worker of magic and a prince among healers," the sahib declared joyfully, once they were well away from the government building. "You will not always be a cook-bearer. I predict great things for your future."

Robi bowed his head modestly. "You are too kind, Sahib."

The American was carrying his new machine, cradling it like a beloved child in his arms. Robi too was eager to help transport it, for it was his duty; but the sahib was so joyous at having rescued it from the Dungeon of the Tax Castle that he could not bring himself to relinquish it. Since it was exceedingly heavy, Robi did not quarrel too much with this affection for it. When a man loves a burden, he must be permitted to bear it.

"How glad I am that you came along with me. How lucky that you were carrying your parcel with remedies."

"It was merely my duty, Sahib. You are too generous."

"Never mind. Your twig and your ginger tea worked after reason, good will, common sense, all else failed. That tax official would not have surrendered the machine to me. He was a fierce opponent, a Bengal tiger, and you tamed him with a mere twig."

"Not a mere twig. *Bel.* A twig from the *bel gacch.* Very salutary for the health. I did not cheat that man, you know. After he drinks quantities of the ginger tea and wears the *bel* two full days, he will be a person of health and vigor. The tree also bears fruit—much like oranges—but, alas, I did not think to bring some along. I do still have one extra bit of the branch in my bundle, Sahib. Would you care to wear it? Delhi air is foul and dangerous; the *bel* will be your guardian."

"Yes, I would be glad to wear it." He indicated that Robi might drop it in the pocket of his bush shirt. Everyone knows that an amulet should be worn next to the skin, but since the sahib had no sacred thread and Robi did not think he would don a waist cord to wear a twig, he kept silent. For Americans, he thought, who knows? The *bel* may work through cloth.

How to describe his exalted feelings at that moment? He was Robi Gangulee Shlemiel Babu who only a short time before had been reduced to ricksha-wallah. Now he was in Delhi, *vaid* to a tax official and to a sahib.

After storing the machine away carefully in the hotel, they had a democratic consultation, a very popular pastime with Americans. It means much fanciful talk before an obvious decision.

"We have finished our business too quickly, Robi. I expected delays, so I booked our tickets for Wednesday. That gives us the whole afternoon and tomorrow with nothing to do. Let's walk over to the Government Tourist Office and see if they can help us exchange our tickets for seats on an earlier train—tonight, maybe."

"We must not return tonight, Sahib."

"Why not?"

"R.P. Mukerjee, the Tagore scholar, rides the train tonight."

"Good point. Let us see what can be done about tomorrow then."

Such a brief stay in Delhi would be a terrific waste, Robi thought.

The squint-eyed clerk behind the Government Tourist Office counter—for a quantity of *annas* Robi discreetly poured into his cupped hands—declared that he could *not* find a suitable booking. He was desolate but they would have to remain in Delhi until their scheduled departure. Such are the trials of mechanical dependence. "In my grandfather's time, one walked," the clerk declared profoundly and Robi had to agree with that.

"I had no idea that trains were so crowded," the sahib said. "Any suggestions, Robi, on how we can best spend our time here?"

A few dozen fine ideas burned like young fires in Robi's mind, but he was too shy to express them.

"You will not think me bold, Sahib, if I make some suggestions?"

"No. I asked you."

"And if they are inappropriate or too costly for a person of my station, you will say so?"

"Robi—stop it."

Robi had a half dozen more protestations ready, but American impatience is destructive to the complexity of relationships.

"Perhaps there is a bus tour of Delhi this afternoon, so that we may admire the greatness of the capital city."

"Fine idea."

"And for tomorrow! Agra is not a long journey, Sahib. I have heard that the trip can be comfortably done in one day. The Taj may be viewed on such an excursion."

"Wonderful." The sahib went back to the counter and that very same squint-eyes exacted further bakshish—that clerk will one day soon be able to buy golden eyeglasses and retire from government service—he would put them, he said, on the tour with the best Hindi-English speaking Guide in Delhi. Leaving in three minutes. They would have to run.

They ran, through the heavy rains to the bus. It was not quite filled; the other passengers, mostly Americans of assorted sizes, shapes, and ages, all seemed to have heavy colds.

If I had brought a whole *bel* tree, Robi thought, and a ricksha full of ginger tea, I could have treated them all.

Most remarkable among the Americans were two brave, aged little ladies, like spiders, all dressed in black even to gloves. These grandmothers were studying a tour book. Also on the bus was a sprinkling of Indian tourists, and in the seat right behind the driver was that paragon, The Guide. He was a mammoth of a Sikh in a heavy yellow rubber coat with a swagger stick under his arm such as British army sahibs carried. He was altogether Mr. Dignified Winston Churchill reincarnated, this Punjabi personage, in his externals, and he chose to speak his welcome address in English only, disregarding Robi and the other Indian passengers. At the Red Fort, he again gave information in English only.

Robi stepped ahead to help the two old American ladies—who insisted on exploring this entire fortress palace of the Moghul emperors surrounded by its incredible walls of slabs of red sandstone. These ancients were soon to be drowned because the rain was storing up inside the Fort like waters in a dam. Robi assisted them and hurried them back, lifting them onto the bus as was his duty to the elderly. They rewarded him with much wet bakshish.

The Guide apparently had no plans to descend from the bus. His yellow rubber coat was an affectation. His procedure was to order the vehicle driven to within sight of a landmark. Then, very briefly he would describe the site and offer dates: "Jumma Masjid, 1658 A.D., built by Shah Jahan, contains a slipper of Mohammed's and a hair of the Prophet."

He was about to lean back comfortably in his safe dry seat and pop a sweet in his mouth when Robi began politely to question him. Was this so? and Who? he inquired. When? and Why? and How much? and Where? and Why not? and

If? and Wouldn't it? and Couldn't they?—and he went on and on with his charming interrogatives until his Hindi-speaking compatriots joined in the game and the Guide was forced to reveal all the history he knew about this location, and to apologize for what he did not know. Which was much. One ancient gentleman, who wished the dimensions of the western side of the Jumma Masjid because he was considering the construction of a similar edifice in Gujerat, was so angered by the Guide's ignorance that he threatened to have the man cashiered. And he could do it, too, for he had relatives in government, high, high up. Very high up.

From then on the Guide was a reformed character. He led them off the bus; he was the first one into the rain, and he spoke at length about each site, *in Hindi first* and then in English.

While they were traveling to each new location, he studied his Guidebook assiduously so that he might be better prepared to lecture to them.

For Robi, the most wonderful stop on the tour was at the simple marble tomb, the *Raj Ghat*, which marks the place where Gandhi had been cremated. Standing in the midst of the beautiful green park was the tomb bearing his last words—"Oh God." This glorious Hindi inscription was blanketed by pilgrims' flowers, a mountain of beauteous colors and blossoms glistening in the rain. The *Raj Ghat* was a place of absolute commemoration; Robi felt that he had come into a holy presence. Quietness overtook him—the sahib too—and the feeling of the great glory of peace.

He did not torment the Sikh further, but rode back to the city silently, his mind inspired by the memory of his beloved Mahatma.

When the sahib gave him two rupees to tip the Sikh with, he rebelled. He would not.

Such a corrupt rascal, to be a government Guide and own a yellow rubber raincoat and then just *sit* on the bus speaking only in English. He was a disgrace to the Ideals of Indian Democracy. A blight. An abomination. How many pure young men all over India—especially in Bengal where they were the purest—would give their hearts to have a chance at his government job with pension! And if hired, would do the job heroically, magnificently, studying history night and day so as to be properly informed when asked a vital detail such as the measurements of the western side of the Jumma Masjid. This illiterate was a criminal and Robi would not pass two rupees into such stained hands!

Of course he could not utter these sentiments aloud to the sahib who was a compulsive bakshish-giver. This was an American racial trait revealed when their army was stationed in India during their great war with Japan and Germany. They were also habitual distributors of chocolate bars, and while the sahib did not have the candy peculiarity, the other pattern was racial and therefore could not be altered.

Blocking the front door of the bus was the Sikh, waiting to bid each of them—*his beloved companions on this delighful peregrination into the triumphant history of Delhi*—a warm good-bye. The man now was shooting off fancy words like a firecracker exhibition on Boxing Day. So many *Namastes* and *Cheerios* came forth he was practically the president of the Anglo-Indian League.

He declared loudly that they *were a spectacularly nice crowd of tourists* and he was *clasping each of them to the bosom of fond memory forever.* The man had no shame; on and on he went.

The sahib slid out of his seat and walked forward. Robi sat, politely urging the two elderly ladies to go ahead of him. He was much concerned with their safety and, as he had to issue many instructions by gesture to them, his sahib was well ahead of him by the time he finally rose.

"Good-bye, Sahib." First the Sikh shook hands and then he hit the sahib's shoulder with the force of a thunderclap striking Ladakh. Fortunately for the American, Robi thought, he is wearing the *bel* which keeps muscles undamaged.

The Sikh gazed deep into sahib's eyes. *Where is my tip?* his intense glance demanded. *Where is my bakshish?*

The sahib had, by now, learned to read eye language pretty well. He merely looked back toward Robi and nodded, signaling to the avaricious Sikh that the wealth of the New World—Columbus's Gold—was still aboard, behind the two old ladies.

The Sikh moved aside and allowed him to descend. The ladies hobbled past with many compliments for the Guide. They dropped much money into his hand.

Robi waited, holding back until they had descended—he did not wish to frighten them by coming too close behind them—and when they cleared the steps, he hastened forward like a man on a sudden urgent errand.

"*N-n-n-n-na-namaskar,*" he whispered, suddenly afflicted with terrible difficulties of speech. All the while he was moving forward and digging frantically in the pocket of his *kurta.* He was almost down the steps when he brought forth a handful of small coins. He thrust them into the greedy out-stretched paw and leaped gracefully out, a most obedient servant in hot pursuit of his departing master.

He did not cast back a single glance, but he had confidence that the Sikh was compelled to concentrate on *his beloved companions in this delighful peregrination* who were closer at hand. Surely Punjabis are adherents of that old adage, "What is gone is gone, gone!"

Next day it was necessary to make their one further pilgrimage to Agra to admire "the most glorious tomb that grief ever raised in memory of love." Of course, it was the Taj Mahal, the tomb of Mumtaz Mahal, Exalted of the Palace, and Mumtaz-ul-Zamana, the Wonder of the Age (all one lady) who was married to the Moghul Emperor Shah Jahan in 1612 when she was twenty-one years old. She bore him fourteen children, then died in childbirth in 1631. Robi found this hard to understand; after fourteen babies, she should have had skill at the task. Women were slow to learn things, he concluded.

The Emperor's hair immediately turned gray—further proof of Robi's theory about aristocratic hair—so great was his grief that the Shah determined to build this monument which would keep her name immortal.

Second Class tickets, Robi had assured the sahib, would provide them with comfortable passage on the train to Agra. It would be foolish to waste rupees on better seats; only the show-offs traveled First Class. Robi was not comfortable in such stiff society.

At six in the morning, carrying lunch boxes courtesy of the Broadway Hotel, they boarded. They sat in a car that had four low, thinly padded benches. The other occupants included five enormous Sikhs—none in a yellow rubber raincoat, Robi noted—four assorted children; a toothless man, his wife and their lovely toothless baby; a grand elderly dame in blue sari and layers of western jewelry, who spread herself immediately over two seats and commenced to read *The Times of India.* On came a handsome young prince of a student in white pants and shirt who looked around at all the people once over his thin nose, and then, dismissing humanity, he crept into his thick book and began to make notes in its margins.

A noisy group of good-natured businessmen in their fifties, all in *dhotis* and bearing great umbrellas, boarded late and rode standing all the way. A lovely sight was one quiet, modest, and grave young woman in a handsome plum sari who sat motionless as a stone carving during the entire trip.

Overhead were three berths; in them lay three worthless youths who had been early-comers and had grabbed the desirable territory and planted their flags. These sybarites were too quick with their nastiness and their witty remarks whenever a fellow passenger required to rest a small lunch-box or two on the end of one of the berths, there being no other place to put it except in said fellow passenger's lap.

The Badmash occupying the berth over the sahib and Robi chose to sit up and swing his feet freely. Since these very large feet reached down just to the eye level of those below, the fields of Uttar Pradesh were viewed by them intermittently between his calluses. Robi was ready to give him blows but the sahib absolutely forbade it. Gandhiji would have embraced the American who was a congenital master of *satyagraha*.

The trip was pleasant indeed. Toward midday it began to get steamy as one might expect, but the atmosphere remained jovial; the businessmen, who were standing, bellowed pleasantries at one another and spat *pan* juice out the open door; the scholar read intently and wrote marvelously small; the matronly dame studied her newspaper, and the parents of the babe played with it quietly.

Since Robi had a scientific mind—that is why he leaned toward medicine—he studied the sign prominently posted on the wall which announced that this car held sixteen adult persons. He then conducted a count; there were thirty-seven people in the car. How wasteful it would have been to obey the sign. They were all quite comfortable. Quite.

Agra at last, and the sahib was the very first pilgrim off the train. Red-in-the-face and weak-in-the-knees, he drank four lemonades in a row, then he whispered to Robi—who had no idea why he was whispering since they did not know anyone there—"We will ride back First Class. I am going to arrange it now."

He walked off, leaving his servant puzzling as he often did about the stamina of Americans; he was convinced that they were so weak because they took beef in large quantities. Surely that was what was corrupting their national blood. If he could get to America and start a movement, he could help them; they needed a *guru*. He could bring them spiritual enlightenment and probably make his fortune doing it.

No matter what the sahib said, Robi knew that Second Class was really very comfortable. One might even say luxurious. He expressed these convictions to the American, who returned with First Class tickets; the only response he got was a groan.

Though Robi urgently reminded him of the corrupt Sikh

and warned him of the consequences, the American insisted that they must hire their guide from the Government Tourist Office, instead of looking for one they could bargain with on the streets of Agra.

This time they were more fortunate; the gods occasionally protect the innocent. For twelve rupees—there is gold in this Guide Business, Robi noted, if a man Live near a Proper Place of History—they obtained the exclusive services of Sahib Golub, an official Guide, though poorly dressed in trousers the color of olives and a frayed white shirt. Guide Golub carried the most imposing briefcase Robi had ever seen, and his first words to the Brahmin were *"Ahimsa* leather, brother, made from a cow that died of senility. I have verified it myself." Robi liked the man at once.

On hearing that the sahib was a scholar, the Guide immediately detailed for them how he too was more a scholar than a mere guide. He had hoped to study ancient history and teach it; it had not been his fortune to be privileged to study it formally in college.

Guide Golub was an interesting example of two men at once. At the sites of official monuments he puffed up and lectured like a toad who had swallowed great history books; otherwise, he was a plain good fellow such as one might confide one's troubles to in a tea shop.

Fatehpur Sikri first, the deserted red sandstone city built by the great Akbar after a priest, Salim Chisti, had prophesied that Akbar would have a son born on this site.

The son obligingly was born and the capital was built.

"Scholars of English history may remember," Guide Golub's book said, "That it was to Fatehpur Sikri that Queen Elizabeth in 1583 sent her letter desiring trading facilities that resulted in the East India Tea Company. The Englishmen who brought the Queen's letter reported that the Indian city was 'much greater than London and very populous' and that they saw 'much merchandise of silk and cloth and precious stones, both rubies and diamonds and pearls.'"

Each building they walked through was a palace. Whenever Akbar wished to play chess, he sat on a throne high above the great courtyard which was laid out in black and white squares. His chess pieces were slave girls.

Those Moghuls were original men! Dangerous original men! So Robi thought, tremendously impressed; he could see that the sahib was affected the same way.

They came upon a religious shrine, the *Tomb of the Saint* which was *sacred to both Hindus and Moslems*! This was most remarkable to Robi, this marble crypt where the priest Salim Chisti was buried under a burial canopy of carved sandalwood and inlaid mother-of-pearl. Robi had never looked upon such beauty. Around the grave was placed a pierced marble screen, again of exquisitely crafted stone, and to this screen came barren women, poor creatures, to attach red threads as they prayed for children. The screen was aglow with red threads.

"Why was the city abandoned?" the sahib wondered, as they wandered through the wide, deserted streets.

Guide Golub inflated himself, and delivered the appropriate lecture with the greatest formality. "Historians offer two theories. Theory Number One is that Akbar moved his court so that the Saint could have peace and quiet. This is the officially accepted explanation which you will find in all the authorized history books. But—"

The man's eyes developed wild lights, flashes and glints of brilliance that come when One Knows the Truth.

—"Theory Number Two, which I and many other Scholarly People adhere to—and about which I have published a small pamphlet at my own expense, in the interest of enlightenment, Donation One Rupee—" He pointed to the imposing-looking briefcase as the repository of this printed wisdom. "Theory Number Two maintains unequivocally that—Akbar ran out of water here."

He was gleeful, rubbing his hands and rumbling and giggling a bit as he expounded this theory with the greatest enthusiasm. "Ten thousand people lived here in Fatehpur Sikri—too many for the water supply—they lived here for thirteen years, then they had to relocate in Agra. It makes sense. All the calculations and five serious statistical tables are set forth in large type in my pamphlet." He paused to contemplate the majestic deserted streets. "What a pity!"

"I am certainly interested in your theory," the sahib said politely.

He would buy a dead horse if someone offered it, Robi thought.

"I would like to buy two copies from you."

"Two, Sahib?" Guide Golub was stunned. Robi understood that the man had probably not sold two altogether since his private printing at his own expense.

"Yes. One for Robi's library and one for mine."

And that is the very spot where Robi's library was born, on that vast deserted street in Fatehpur Sikri. It has grown much since its humble beginning. In the bookstore in Delhi he purchased his own copy of the *Atharva Veda*, at great cost, as well as several other more modestly priced medical pamphlets. On the trip home he acquired, in addition, 47 Timetables, 59 Tour Guides, 7 Menus, 3 Public Notices of Hunger Strikes and assorted other printed materials, and since then he has been a diligent collector of reading matter. A library is a serious thing, and Robi worked hard at his.

Having exchanged money for pamphlets, they were ready to stop for lunch. They moved off to a suitable flat rock. The tourists opened their lunchboxes and Guide Golub brought forth two bananas and an orange from his briefcase.

Immediately, the silent grandeur of the distant past fled. All the flies in India, as well as those of Pakistan, Tibet, Nepal, Ceylon, Indonesia, and China—and Robi recognized a new and independent strain from Bangladesh—responded to the scent of the Broadway Hotel lunchboxes. Beggars rose up magically from nowhere to surround them, moving in slowly. A street entertainer with two monkeys in ragged gold velvet organized his show in front of them, prodding the poor tattered creatures to dance. Hungry children assembled nearby and watched as the visitors tried, simultaneously, to chase flies and peel eggs.

From nowhere, a wet-eyed young beggar woman wearing yellowed rags and green glass bangles, her hair a greasy tumbled mass, fell before the sahib and clutched his shoes, babbling at him.

"What is wrong, Robi?"

"She desires your scraps, Sahib."

A battle plan had to be formulated at once. "I will keep the flies and beggars off, Sahib, while you eat first. Then I will eat," Robi suggested.

"I am no longer hungry," the sahib said. "You and the Guide may eat my share or give it away." He seated himself on a stone, shut his eyes, and rested his head in his hands.

Robi pitied him. Beef, beef; he was weak because all those years he had chewed on the Mother Cow.

Guide Golub and Robi began to eat, but they had not much appetite either. This worried Robi. Perhaps his association with the Americans was damaging his blood strength, too. Since he could not afford to believe such a troublesome thought, he put it aside.

They, too, soon abandoned the remains to the many beggars.

On to the Taj!

Now, a Valmiki, a Kalidasa, or a Rabindranath is needed to write the description; ordinary words are dull stones where precious gems should be set.

Their first glimpse was of a delicate beauty, the pure whiteness rising from a platform to form a perfect pear-shaped dome. Four smaller domes clustered below it like babes, miniatures of the greater Mother. The slender minarets at the corners of the platform—closed because, Guide Golub detailed for them, these were such poetically beautiful suicide sites that this one and that one and every other one had jumped off them—the stately terraces and the beautifully inlaid walks cutting through the landscaped gardens, were all truly reflected in the great clear pool, and all were consumed by the hungry viewer in his very first glance.

"It is the most beautiful building in the entire world," Robi exclaimed to the sahib. "More beautiful, I am sure now, than that building in New York City that I have heard much about."

"Which building?"

"The one so tall it pierces the sky with a sharp metal finger, and once it challenged a great airplane to a duel and the airplane lost."

National pride did not concern the sahib much. He was amazingly amiable when challenged. "The Empire State Building. You're right. This is more beautiful. I think we might conclude that the Shah was fond of his wife. This is a tribute to love."

Guide Golub nodded most agreeably, but Robi discounted this assent because the day's outing was nearly completed and he knew the man had bakshish on his mind.

"No doubt, Sahib, she was the beginning of the inspiration. But afterwards—it was all men. Women can be beginnings—like mothers." Robi stopped, awed at the depth of his own thinking. "But ask yourself, who did it? The architects, the designers, the artists, the craftsmen. Without *men* we would have no Taj Mahal!"

As they made their way out, these profundities preoccupied him, and before he said good-bye to Guide Golub, he spoke to him about the details and problems of printing a small pamphlet of one's opinions. Robi learned much which he carefully recorded in a copybook, which he bought to mark down certain plans for his future

"Welcome back. I hope you didn't drink any unboiled water."

How pleasing it was to hear the familiar worried voice uttering its usual message of liquid madness. For Robi, it was like having a mother of his own again. Being the source of concern of another human being was a delightful luxury.

Both travelers were dusty and weary but exhilarated. The sahib immediately bathed and then went into his office to try out his new machine.

Robi bathed, pouring bucket after bucket of water on himself as he scrubbed away the dirt of the great distances. As he entered his kitchen and looked around him, he was astonished to see that after all the hundreds of kilometers he had traveled and after all the adventures that had befallen him, the kitchen was exactly the same. Many wooden matches were missing, his sharp eyes noted, and the salt sack had been pillaged. That Laljit was incorrigible; Robi resolved to shout at the sweeper that very night. But otherwise, the dented pots on the shelf; the spatula, the rice spoon and the whisk on their nails in the plastered walls; the *chulha* and the stove, the coal and the dung cakes, were all there. Oddly, the world was unaffected by the incredible events that had occurred in his life.

With grandeur on his mind—but no fresh meat on hand—Robi prepared a vegetarian feast: potato chops stuffed with curried peas, rice and *dal*, fried eggplant slices, chick peas, and fresh made *jelibe* for dessert. He was thanking the sahib for the trip, using the occasion of this meal as his means. He put several bouquets of marigolds on the table in water glasses, and he went to much trouble to set the electric fan strategically so it would blow away flies and not the food.

Memsahib gave Robi many compliments as she ate with good appetite from the variety of dishes. It appeared that, while the Sen family were most kind and hospitable, the cooking in that household was not anywhere near the consummate artistry that Robi achieved. Not anywhere near it! In the Sen household! Robi was very close to bursting with joy.

The sahib began to tell all their adventures, allowing Robi to add details and dramatize the critical events: how they listened to and were prisoners of the Tagore fanatic; how the ice-water *dacoit* invaded their room and tricked them most outrageously; how Robi heroically rescued the new machine from the Dungeon of the Tax Dragon using ginger tea and *bel* twig as his weapons; how the corrupt Sikh Guide had given them such a poor tour of Delhi, and how the Good Guide Golub had modestly introduced them to the real beauty of Agra, and truthfully explained to them exactly what had happened at Fatehpur Sikri.

"Robi—" the memsahib remembered—"when you have taken your meal and then finished up in the kitchen, walk over to see Bahadur. He was here this morning, very mysterious—he said he had something of importance to say to you whenever you had the time to hear it. He wouldn't tell me another word."

"I will go, Memsahib. Soon."

Robi ran towards the Healer's house. Never did he come out onto the roads at this hot hour of day, for the sun was injurious—it dried the brain—but he was anxious to know the news. Good or bad? In his hand he held a small packet, a gift he had bought in Delhi for Bahadur.

As he approached the modest mud building—the Healer, a public vegetarian who secretly ate meat, and kept a radio and an electric razor hidden in his back room—believed that he kept the confidence of his village trade by appearing to live in the most traditional way; Robi was astonished to note the silence, the absolutely deserted quality of the place. Usually an assemblage of sick folk in varying drastic conditions waited in this small yard. Today there was no one. He has cured them all, Robi thought sadly, and there will be no one under the pipal tree any more.

The shutters were fastened against the sun.

And the door was closed! Now this was strange, for the Healer liked to have Bahadur tell it around the marketplace that his door was open twenty-five hours a day to the sick. What could have occurred?

Robi crept up to the side where he knew Bahadur's sleeping pallet was placed beneath the window. He waited, summoning courage before he made a sound, because if he woke the Healer there would be Dire Consequences.

"Bahadur—" he whispered softly. "Bahadur? Nepali?"

Not a sound from within. The house was a crypt.

"Bahadur?" Robi fastened his ear to the crack below the shutter, and closed his eyes so he could concentrate on sounds.

"Rrrrrrrrrrrrrkh!" Such a monstrous roar came from behind him that he jumped forward, banging his brow on the rim of the shutter. Bahadur was right behind him, laughing and jumping with glee. "Robibabu, what did you think? Did you think I was a demon?"

"You are a demon."

Bahadur noticed the package. "What are you carrying?"

"It was a gift for you, Badmash! But I don't think I will give it to you now. I will keep it for myself. You don't deserve it."

"We will see." Laughing, Bahadur grabbed for it and Robi fell in with the game, avoiding him and running away. For some minutes they dashed about in the yard this way, one pursuing and one pursued, until Robi was winded and Bahadur cornered him and forced the package from his hand.

It was a small model of the Taj, complete with blue reflecting pool, encased in a plastic bubble. When the model was turned upside down, a silvery snowstorm fluttered within the bubble. Bahadur was enchanted by it, and Robi was now a bit wistful that he had not bought one for himself as well.

While they were admiring the toy, it came to Robi that he did not yet understand the situation. Bahadur seemed to have free time now—these were not his off-hours—and he was fooling around with a friend right in the Healer's own front yard. The Healer must have gone off on a trip somewhere.

"Bahadur, what has happened? Where is your Healer? Has he gone off on a trip? This is the first time I see his front door closed."

Bahadur was watching the miniature snowstorm. "He has gone on a trip far away. Far, far away, Robibabu. My healer is dead."

"Dead?" This news stunned Robi. Impossible. The man had been perfectly alive only three days before. Robi had gone off to Delhi, and now the man was dead.

"How did it happen?"

Bahadur tapped his chest. "His heart just stopped."

"But he had heart pills."

"Robibabu, I will tell you a secret that no one knows. And you must swear you will never tell. Never."

"I swear."

Bahadur came very close. "The heart pills were missing. For a whole day we searched, he and I, and none could be found. Before I could get to the apothecary for more pills, he was gone."

"That is too sad. What can have happened to the pills?"

Bahadur looked very pious. "That man had many enemies, you know. He took much money for healing and often he did not help the sick—so anyone could have sneaked in and stolen them."

"By covetousness sin, by sin death." Robi pronounced his stern judgment.

"I am only sorry that we had bad words on that last day," Bahadur said, shaking the small Taj again so the silver would float down. "The Healer was an unjust man and he accused me of robbing him of rupees. And then when the pills were missing he said I even took those away, to sell. He was a harsh, difficult man. I never took his rupees—a few pice on the marketing, yes, but no *rupees*. He was no American, easily fooled; he counted every grain of rice. Only a fool would have stolen rupees from him, and I am not a fool."

Robi believed him. "I know you are sorry he is dead."

"One does not know the worth of teeth while they last," Bahadur declared gravely.

"Now what is to happen here?" Robi pointed to the closed-up house.

"That is what I wanted to see you about. Yesterday the Healer's family came and took him off to the burning ghat. Six aunts arrived from the village in their buffalo cart, and they cleaned every possession out of the house, the radio, the razor, the cooking wares, and clothing. Even the few cupfuls of rice in the storeroom. They were witches with penetrating eyes, seeing every item and seizing it, no matter how small its value. Bahadur's eyes began to sparkle. "I managed to hide a few insignificant objects before they came." He stopped talking and looked around carefully. Not a person was in sight; it was the hottest time of day. "I have a present for you, Doctorbabu." From under his shirt he lifted—a gleaming silver disc on a strong neckwire—a stethoscope.

Robi gasped. It was beautiful—and he knew how to use one from the early years of his life, when his grandfather and then his father had taught him. "How did you do it? Didn't the aunts demand it?"

"Yes, they did and they called me thief when they could not find it. But I said their nephew was a stingy suspicious man, always frightened of being robbed so he hid or he buried all his valuables in strange places and therefore I could not tell where his stethoscope was, but they were free to tear open the bedding and dig up the yard."

"Did they believe you?"

"Of course not. But they didn't find the stethoscope."

"Bahadur—" Robi was speechless with gratitude.

"We are partners," Bahadur said graciously. "You have given me a Taj, so I must give you a present too."

"Dare I wear it? People will wonder where I got it. There will be talk."

"You will wait until the Americans go. Then you can wear it and say that you bought it in Delhi. Everyone knows you were in Delhi. I told them."

"What will you do now, Bahadur? Where will you go?"

"That is why I told the memsahib to send you, Robibabu. I have been thinking since this happened—the Americans are leaving in a few weeks so you too will be without work or a place to sleep. This small house is now empty. It costs twelve rupees a month and is already known all over the district as the house of a Healer...."

Robi understood at once, and was delighted. "You think that we can receive enough presents from healing the sick to pay such a rent and live here?"

"Robibabu—" Bahadur's smile was sheer confidence. "You leave it to me. I have already ordered that a sign be painted for the front of the house. It is to be a large sign, blue letters on a yellow background, the whole thing bordered in red. There will be Bengali printing, very large, and underneath the same words in English, but smaller."

"What will it say?"

"What it must say. 'MEDICAL CENTER OF INDIA'S RUHR!'"

And there would have to be a smaller sign on the post by the outside door, Robi resolved privately, a sign such as the doctors in Delhi had, and it would read "Robi Gangulee Shlemiel, Healer."

*I*n his kitchen, Robi chanted a catalogue of household goods that would be his once the Americans departed:

> Water buckets, sweeping brooms
> Tablewares, rice pot
> Coffeepot, other pots
> Cups, plates, bowls
> Coal stove, coal
> Beds, pillows
> Sheets, netting
> Bottles, openers
> Tins, grindstone
> Clotheslines, torches
> Locks, keys
> Beautiful electric fan...

All would be his to keep or sell or give away. Every time he handled a dish or any implement that was part of his inheritance, he fondled it tenderly.

In Calcutta they were already anxiously awaiting the monsoons, but Asansol would not get the rains till much later. The Americans were eager to depart; Asansol was unbearably hot, the nights no different than the days. Bedclothes were soggy; nets were no longer necessary at night because even the mosquitoes had been overpowered by the heat. People were irritable, perpetually sweaty, their throats parched.

Robi, fond of his employers and grateful to them for so much, now had a small medical practice that would keep him afloat, so he was not heartsick at their imminent departure. Life was a progression of experiences, and all men had to move on. He would never forget them and their peculiar kindness; they had opened this world to him. He already had their address in New York City carefully recorded in his notebook, so that if he ever got there he could find them. He had their telephone number too. Actually, he was a bit restless in anticipation of their going because he was eager to wear the stethoscope which he had wrapped in a soft cloth and hidden in his room.

It was midday and most of the people of the district were already taking their rest. This was Robi's intention too, once he finished clearing up, after the large lunch. He took longer in the kitchen these days because he was very careful not to break or damage his valuables-to-be.

In the front office behind bamboo blinds, the sahib sat listening to the sweet voices of Bengali village children speaking on his machine. The memsahib, her head protected against the sun by a close-woven kerchief, at Robi's admonition, had walked out to post letters to America. She would be the only walker on the road at this hour; stubbornly, she refused to be governed by the sun.

"*Jao! Jao!*" Robi heard her scream. And again, "*Jao!*"

There was terror in that scream, not annoyance at a beggar or slight fear at the gestures of a passing madwoman. Terror!

Carefully, Robi set the rice pot on the stove. Then he ran. The sahib, too, was running.

There she lay on the road, a heap of blue cloth just a little distance from the house, with a great, filthy, white-gray dog—the size of a full-grown sheep—attacking her bare leg.

Robi knew in his heart that this was her retribution for walking about half-naked. Grabbing up a stick, he ran toward the dog shouting, "*Jao, kukur! Jao!*" Sahib, too, was bellowing and waving a pole as he ran forward.

The dog looked up at them and then bounded away along the road.

They reached her at the same moment. She lay in the dust gasping and crying with terror, the only time Robi had seen her express such strong feeling. Sahib held her to him and tried to comfort her.

Robi kneeled and looked at the leg. The dog had chewed the flesh on the back of her knee and scratched her, long stripes of red down to the ankle. Blood and dirt and hanging skin were all intermingled.

"Let us lift her, Sahib, and help her inside." Robi offered his shoulder, and, with the sahib taking the other side, they managed to raise her up off the road. She was not a heavy lady and she became courageous almost at once. It astonished Robi to see that she had such inner strength. Unexpected dimensions in a meat-eating woman.

Her sobbing had stopped. Whimpering now, softly, and leaning heavily on them both, she managed to hop inside. They helped her onto a chair in the inner yard. "The dog must be caught alive," the sahib said, as he brought out his first aid box and began to take out cotton and antiseptic and bandages, "so that we can tell if it is mad. Robi, I'm going to clean up the memsahib's leg now, and then I'm going to drive her to the doctor. You get some local men and try to catch the dog if you can. Be very careful for yourselves. Tell any man who helps you that I will give many rupees reward if the dog is captured alive."

"Sahib —" Robi began shyly—"You are family to me. I will suck the poison out and say *mantras* for the memsahib."

"Thank you, Robi." The sahib was brusque. "But we must go to a doctor to get this cauterized and tended to. It probably requires many stitches. And you must try at once to catch the dog."

"We will catch the dog, Sahib, I promise. I will call some of the smart local men who are taking their rest now. I will call Bahadur with the others. The dog will be waiting for you when you return."

For more than an hour the volunteers chased the dog. Five local men—Robi with a sack and a stick, and the others with sticks and rocks—hunted the dog across the broken landscape.

They trapped him finally in a rocky junction near the washermen's pond. By then he had already bitten a water buffalo, a donkey, and two goats. "Be careful, boys," Robi reminded them. "The sahib requires him alive." They had to stone him, for no one could approach him without great danger to self, but they tried to do it moderately, only enough to stun him. He stood against the flat rocks, wild-looking, barking and howling, and rolling his white eyes.

"He is mad," Bahadur judged. "Mad with the heat." Bahadur took careful aim and stoned him with accuracy.

When the beast lay down finally, after being pelted for a long time, the hunters surrounded the place and moved in slowly, Robi and another holding the sack open like a great soft cave.

Closer they came, and closer, cautiously, ever more slowly. There was an evil steamy stench about the animal. They paused. Bahadur aimed a small stone and threw it. The dog lifted its head and looked but did not try to stand.

"He cannot stand," Bahadur said. "We have him."

All together, as smoothly as Rajputs on a tiger hunt long ago, the group cooperated; swiftly, with flat boards as shovels and poles as prods, they engineered the dog into the sack. With care they roped it tightly and knotted the rope, then all together—for it was heavy—they dragged it back to the Lotus Bungalow and set it on the veranda for the sahib. They squatted in the front yard now, all of them, relieved, chattering and laughing, reenacting parts of the chase, hunters triumphant with their success. The Landrover drove up less than an hour afterwards. The memsahib, her face the color of rice powder, her leg bandaged from ankle to thigh, limped inside, nodding a silent greeting to the men. She cast her eyes away from the laden sack.

"Sahib, we have captured the dog alive," Robi reported joyfully

"I can never tell you how grateful I am." The sahib took out his wallet and gave each man *four* rupees. A fortune for an afternoon's work. Robi hoped that each would remember that it was he who had done the recruiting for this job, he who had gone to their houses in the hot sun and summoned them.

"The animal is injured, Sahib, for we were forced to stone him to weaken him. But he is in the sack, alive."

The sahib wanted to have a look at the brute. Arming themselves again with their boards and rocks, the men ringed the dangerous area. Robi opened the sack and stepped back immediately.

The creature was inert. Robi prodded the sack and the great ugly head wiggled slightly; the eyes opened once, and then the head fell limp. The dog was dead.

"I am sorry, Sahib." Robi felt terrible. It had been a sacred trust.

The sahib was upset. He put his fingers to his eyes and rubbed hard. "It's not your fault, Robi—but now I have to see if there's a laboratory in the area that can examine the dead dog and find out if it was rabid—mad."

"It was mad, Sahib." Bahadur assured him of it. "It bit a water buffalo, a donkey, and two goats after it bit the memsahib."

"I have to be sure. The doctor says there's a problem getting vaccine. And even if we do manage to get it, it might not be pure. And even if it is pure, the shots are so painful—fourteen in the stomach, that if there's a chance—" He was too discouraged to finish.

"In my village back home we just take the dog-bite child—usually it is a child—down to the sacred pond and bathe him," one of the men said.

"And in my home we had a holy man who sucked the poison from the wounds," another remembered. "My baby sister was bitten when she was very young. Two years old."

"And she recovered and was fine?" the sahib asked.

"No, she died, Sahib. Not of dog-bite. Of fever, afterwards."

"I will take the carcass to the government hospital. Robi, please stay here with the memsahib. She will probably sleep soon; the doctor gave her some sleeping medicine."

Bahadur cancelled the hours under the pipal tree, telling all who passed how Robi was caring for the memsahib's dog-bite wounds personally. Word spread through the district about the remarkable Bengali *vaid*, so skilled that even the Americans trusted his medicine. The memsahib's misfortune enhanced Robi's reputation and bolstered the whole area's national pride.

So one man's ruin is another's rainy season.

The Sahib returned unsuccessful. Proper facilities for examining the dog were not available. If the American could get the dog's head cut off, and pack it in quantities of ice, and ship it at once to Calcutta, then perhaps tests would be possible. The technicians were truly sorry but there was nothing they could do.

Laljit came to sweep. Robi recounted all the afternoon's events and told him to get rid of the carcass, which was already stinking up the entire compound, at once. Laljit, sorry for these strangers who were always so nice to him, obliged without a word of protest, though the job was a heavy and unpleasant one. It did not occur to him, this one time, to ask the sahib for bakshish.

The memsahib was asleep. Laljit sat on the veranda to watch the bungalow while the sahib, Robi by his side, began to drive to various administrators and hospitals in the district, trying to obtain the vaccine. The kind doctor, who had cleansed and stitched the memsahib's wounds, had volunteered to give the shots if the sahib could requisition the proper vaccine.

All through the hours of the afternoon they drove from hospital to compound to administrative office. Each time there was a perfectly good reason why the vaccine could not be had. There was none on hand; it was not fresh; it belonged to the government, shots could only be had in the clinic, and there was already a long clinic waiting list.

Robi had never seen the American so disturbed. He sat in the truck, leaning on the wheel, his face in his hands. "I really don't know what to do next, Robi," he confessed. "I just don't know what to do next."

"Perhaps the District Magistrate will help."

"What has he to do with vaccine? The medical people control it."

"The heat of the sun can be borne, but the heat of the sand heated by the sun cannot be borne." Robi quoted softly. "These petty officials cannot be tolerated, Sahib. We must go to the High Authority, the man with the Power. That is the way things are done. Let us try."

The District Magistrate was an uncorruptible brilliant man, much admired in the district. Though he was an ICS appointee from Madras, he had taken the trouble to learn Bengali which he spoke mellifluously, much to the pleasure of the people he governed. He heard the sahib out, then— coolly, efficiently and with great kindness to the American— he tracked down pure fresh vaccine.

When the technician on the telephone—who had turned the two petitioners away earlier saying their request was impossible—protested to the District Magistrate that there was, after all, a certain procedure to be followed in the requisitioning of said vaccine, and that the violation of this procedure in the proposed aforesaid manner would lead directly to fascism, communism, and then anarchy, all inimical to the glorious democracy under which they flourished, the District Magistrate shouted at him to stop at once.

"My driver will be there in half an hour to pick up enough duck serum for the proper treatment of the American lady. You are to have it packed in ice and ready. That is an order!" He hung up.

He made little of what he had just done for them, though the sahib thanked him repeatedly. He promised to send the vaccine on for cold storage to the nearby hospital where it would be easily available to the doctor who was treating the patient, whenever he required it.

"You must forgive our bureaucracy," he said. "We have no proper staff to work with, and therefore people at the top of agencies—like myself—have to give their attention to trivialities." He sighed. "You know the written word has become discounted in modern India. Letters, memoranda, notes are all filed artfully away, but to get something done one must use personal contacts. That is where much of my time is wasted."

He saw them to their vehicle and wished the lady a speedy recovery. He would come by himself, he said, to visit her.

Never had Robi set his eyes on a man more fit to rule. He was a prince. Sahib agreed.

Weary, but ever so relieved and happy, they climbed into the truck to return home. Sahib paused before turning the key, then he spoke, and Robi recognized at once that this was an apology to him. "Robi, we had to get the wounds cleansed and stitched at once, so I could not accept your kind offer when you made it to suck the poison out and say *mantras*. Now the leg is cleaned and bandaged so the sucking is unnecessary—and tomorrow the shots will begin. But if you would say *mantras* for the memsahib, I would be grateful."

Robi pitied him. He was a good man but abysmally ignorant about so many aspects of life, and particularly about medicine. It was fortunate that he had the large first aid box filled with jars and tubes to help protect him from illness. Otherwise, how could he have survived?

"Sahib," he said gently, "*mantras* without sucking do not work."

Epilogue

Majumdar is having a seizure!

Robi sits high in a ricksha. In his hand he holds very carefully his fine black plastic case which contains his instruments: a thermometer, a hypodermic, and a stethoscope, along with one fresh portion of liquid expressed from cow dung and mixed with honey.

Earlier, he had calculated the proper ingredients and his assistant had prepared the remedy.

In his mouth is a fragrant *pan* and he sucks the juices with much pleasure; the lime and the betel leaf and the spices are teasing to his tongue. *Pan* is his single vice.

Ordinarily he takes his sleep during this hour of the day, for the dust of airless noon in this mining and steel-milling district chokes a man. The old, the sick, and often the very young expire unexpectedly here, and mostly during the hot hours. Robi understands this very well.

He is on the road now because of the emergency summons. Majumdar, chief landholder of Vishnapur village—two kilometers from the MEDICAL CENTER—who suffers from the chronic disease of the blood, aggravated by gluttony, is having a severe attack. He cannot breathe and has already fallen down twice. It took five strong villagers to lift him onto the *charpoy* where he lies now, waiting for the Healer.

Most clients do not send for Robi. They come on foot to his MEDICAL CENTER OF INDIA'S RUHR for they are too poor to pay ricksha money. But Majumdar has vast wealth. His gift—discreetly presented to Bahadur, of course, and unacknowledged by the *vaid*—will be in cash rather than in eggplants and cabbages. Though Robi is a strict vegetarian these days, who does not even eat eggs lest they be fertilized (for then he would be taking life, which is a sin), he prefers Bahadur to accept cash gifts rather than vegetables.

Having just taken his meal of curried cabbage, vegetable *samosas*, rice and *dal*, and finished it off with fresh *rasgullas* in thick syrup, Robi was about to enjoy his rest when the Vishnapur boy came on his bicycle with the message: MAJUMDARJI HAS AN ATTACK. HE CANNOT TAKE AIR THROUGH HIS NOSE, AND THERE IS A POUNDING LIKE THUNDERBOLTS IN HIS BRAIN!

This is the second time this month for Majumdar. While so many of his countrymen are wasting away in hunger, he chokes to death of luxury.

Robi, today, is clad in handsome white *kurta* and spotless *dhoti*, sandals of the softest *ahimsa* leather, copper bracelets on his arms and all the appropriate body amulets. Everyone, seeing him, clearly understands that these are only his working clothes. For holidays and *pujas* he has a Kashmiri chest filled with exquisite *dhotis* and *kurtas*. Of the finest cloth, some embroidered and some puckered and sewn in the latest fashion. He owns a Swiss wristwatch and three pens, one blue, one red, and one black, and he is the possessor of an excellent English torch for lighting the way on night errands. His umbrella is of the finest English make. Two coats and a shawl of softest lamb's wool complete his wardrobe. He does not really need the second coat but he has it because he remembers all the cold winters of his life. A man never knows when he may be without a coat again.

Robi enjoys visiting the village though at this time of the day the trip is inconvenient.

Majumdar has a niece, an orphan, living in his household, Susila by name, and Robi has noticed the girl's modest demeanor as she helps her aunt with the chores. She is a tall girl, almost as tall as Robi himself, and she carries herself as straight as a young bamboo plant. She is dusky-skinned, but no one would call her really dark. Whenever he has seen her, Robi has noticed her neat shining hair and her fresh face.

Last time he was summoned, when Majumdar had an attack, he looked up from listening to Majumdar's heart with his stethoscope and caught the girl watching him worshipfully. Quickly, she cast her eyes down and moved away, but there was a lovely, darkening blush to her complexion as she went from the sickroom.

A poor Brahmin girl with blossoms and cobwebs for her dowry; that was surely the single reason she had not been married long before.

Robi would have to have their astrological charts computed properly, but he felt in his heart that they would be propitious. Majumdar, he knew, would not part easily with any wealth. Still—to have the healer readily accessible in the family so to speak, he might be willing to give the girl some gold jewelry and a few household goods.

And a wedding! Robi was resolute. He would insist on a huge village wedding. He had no family of his own to attend, but Majumdar had five hundred wealthy kinsmen who would come from as far away as Bihar and Uttar Pradesh, decorated with gold and shining gems, and they would all bring costly presents.

And he, Robi, beautifully dressed in a white satin *dhoti* and wearing a tall ornamented crown, would drive slowly up the road that night, in a large hired taxi under the arches of leaves and lanterns to the village where the streets would be filled with waiting crowds. A band of musicians would play joyously: drums and gongs and bagpipes would carry through the air of the country night.

He would leave the taxi and be greeted and honored by her male relatives, all clad properly in *dhotis*. The maids from Majumdar's house would come forth to question him.

"Why are you here? Why have you come?"

He would tell them. "I have heard there is a girl here, and I have come to marry her."

The wedding would begin; there would be a beautifully decorated altar with a place for her to sit and another for him, and colorful flowers all over and oil lamps burning.

Her male relatives would carry her to her place; she, her hair loose, her arms braceleted, her face hidden, would keep her head buried in her arms throughout the sacred ceremony.

The pundit would pray and they would repeat certain prayers at his instruction, and they would drop *ghee* and scatter water. They would be united when the saffron *sari* draped over her was tied to his upper garment. Her female relatives would conceal the couple by holding up another saffron *sari*, and he would apply *sindoor* to his wife's parting of her hair and to her forehead.

Then they would rise, and he, behind her with his arms around hers and his hands on top of her hands, would lead her seven times around the altar, both of them stopping to rub their feet on the ceremonial grindstone placed there. Then they would go into a room where, for the rest of the night, her female relatives would sit with them and tease them and make jokes. How merry they would be!

Outside in the great courtyard there would be feasting in their honor; everyone sitting down to curried fish—Majumdar was no vegetarian, but Robi would not permit meat at his wedding feast. They would compromise with fish—and papaya chutney, *dhoi*, *pulao*, *lucis*, eggplants, cabbage, *rasgullas*. All night the feasting would go on in honor of Robi and his bride.

Then he would take her away with him, to be his wife and keep his house. And they would live together peacefully, for he could see that she was an obedient girl and he would be kind to her. He, too, had once been an orphan dependent upon an uncle. And if the gods were good, they would have many children, all as beautiful as she.

Robi does not need movies. In his mind he is entertained vividly and endlessly by his future.

He studies the coolie's bare feet. Slap slap slap they go against the abrasive road; rocks and glass and dung and weeds lie in wait but the feet cannot afford to take notice. Slap slap slap.

Robi glances across at his servant. "Bahadur—tell the coolie to hurry. Majumdar's illness will not wait for idle feet."

Immediately, Bahdur leans forward to chastise the ricksha-wallah who is his countryman, Ram. When the coolie begins to protest the heat of the day and the condition of the road, Bahadur's eyes flash like oil lamps. "*Chup!*" he chides. "Doctorbabu is hurrying to save a life."

Bahadur still maintains the fierce manner of the warrior, the Gurkha, though he is clad now in immaculate white bush shirt and trousers of excellent drill cloth. On his feet are black patent-leather shoes which pain him continually, yet for the sake of style he wears them on all outside calls. Once home in the MEDICAL CENTER he dons sandals. He has stopped going barefoot altogether and the calluses are disappearing from his feet. He reeks now of coconut oil and heavy scents and tobacco and palm wine. He is more western man than Hindu.

Bahadur is both very ignorant and very smart. It is an unbeatable combination. Robi knows that Bahadur understands men better than he, and it is for this reason, particularly, that he values the Nepali as partner. Privately, Robi has always felt that the Nepali was an unworthy associate. Once, he offered to teach Bahadur the Bengali alphabet so that he might be able to read and write—and therefore might raise himself a bit—but Bahadur mocked the offer.

"No, Robibabu, I am the assistant and you are the *vaid*. If you teach me too much, I will get to be too smart. Then there will be trouble between us."

This answer came of sloth, but Robi knew that he was

right. While he could never learn enough to be a good *vaid* or even a herbalist, he could certainly learn enough to fake it.

So Robi, reader of the *Ramayana* and the *Vedas*, lover of learning, is content to remain in partnership with this clever illiterate man.

On Bahadur's wrist is a watch, and in his pocket a pen though he cannot write. All he uses the pen for is to draw pictures, naked ladies and men mating in as many ways as the *Kama Sutra* depicts, perhaps more ways. Sometimes he draws a female with breasts like udders, or a man with grotesque private parts like a victim of elephantiasis. He does these drawings on the paper sacks in the kitchen, the sacks that hold lentils and salt. Whenever Robi sees them, he scolds, "Bahadur, do not do this evil drawing. It profanes our house."

Then Bahadur teases him. "Robibabu, the sacred temples are holy. Is it not so?"

"Of course it is so."

"They are full of such drawings and statues. Is it not so?"

"I have never been to the great temples."

"But you know it is so."

"How can I deny it?"

"These cannot be evil pictures then, for evil pictures would not be kept in holy places."

Confounded by the Nepali's cleverness, Robi is silent and annoyed. He comforts himself by remembering the adage: However you oil a pariah dog's tail, it will never be straight.

Bahadur has taken to visiting the mud-walled tea shop with the tin roof again. For many months he avoided that section of the road entirely; Padmini, his countrywoman, who lived there with her mother, had betrayed him with Fat Assim and had given him a sickness for which he needed shots. His jealousy of her had caused him to fight Assim and so to lose his job with the Americans. But that was long past.

The American couple and their machine were gone now, on a big airplane, back to their land of unlimited wealth and undisciplined wives.

Remember what she said to Senbabu about Gandhi? Remember the water boiling? Remember the light bulb? Late into the nights Robi and Bahadur would reminisce about these two kind but foolish people who had come, like voyagers from a mythical kingdom, bringing their strange customs and beliefs and a whole other way of life to the district.

Robi recalled Guide Golub and what he had read them at Fatehpur Sikri about the English coming; for more than three hundred years these Europeans had been introducing their strange ways to India—but India had always successfully resisted. "We are stronger than they, Bahadur. Much stronger. It is the beef that weakens them," Robi asserted positively at the end of each of these discussions.

Right after the Americans went, the partners began to set up their clinic. First Robi insisted upon whitewashing the entire inside of the little rented house. Bahadur went along with this project, but all the while he worked, he grumbled and was skeptical. "Robibabu, a *vaid* does not have to worry so much about whiteness and cleanness. He can do the same work wearing rags and ashes. In fact, the country people are more accustomed to that. A little ash is very holy and is comforting to see—and to receive."

Robi was indignant. "I will mix the old and the new methods and all who wish to may come. I know the ancient way to cure ailments, but a few good things have been discovered since then. He tapped his beloved stethoscope— which he slept with each night—and pointed to the new thermometer he had purchased. "I will use all."

Together they cleaned the yard and planted flowers along the border, for this was where the patients would wait, under the old trees. The front room was designated as the office, and the back room became their living quarters. The Americans' possessions furnished the house comfortably, and still there was much left over which they sold for a large profit. "Americans crowd their houses so —" Robi observed— "when they have finished buying there is no room to live." He, himself, bought six nicely framed scenes from the

Ramayana, beautifully bright and heartening, and he hung them on the white walls. The office was now ready for patients.

And they came.

With Bahadur's imagination and narrative talent working full time, word spread through the district that Robi had incredible healing powers. Tales were told in the shops and over the vegetable stalls of how he had cured the American woman of rabies when she was already foaming at the mouth; how he had aided a fallen Majumdar on the road, a man he didn't even know at the time; how he had miraculously happened to be right next to a child who was choking on a crumb one morning and he put his finger down her throat and retrieved the crumb, and said a *mantra* and saved her; how even the great Senbabu, known to use western doctors, condescended to stop by one night with a bad toothache, his face swollen like a baboon's, and Robi had given him instant relief with a drop of cinnamon oil and the proper *mantra.*

So they are prospering nicely.

Bahadur walked to the tea stall one morning early when he knew Padmini would be gone to market for sugar and other staples. The old crone, her mother, was there squatting on the ledge, chewing *pan,* and watching her kettle steam. She was polite to him this day, full of "How are you?" and "Fellow countryman," and there was even a "my son" or two scattered like seeds to bear fruit. Bahadur answered her in monosyllables. He drank his tea in a most aloof manner, smashed his clay cup, and paid and walked on. Next time he came, the old woman urged him to take an extra spoonful of sugar in his tea, never mind that sugar was costly; he was her compatriot doing big work with the *vaid.* He managed to keep a grave look while he was there, but he broke up with laughter when he described the scene later. "Robibabu, she treated me like I was her father's elder brother, that old lady. 'Take more sugar, Bahadur. Take a bit more.'"

"They are bad women, Bahadur. Stay away from them."

"They are like me—not bad, only poor," Bahadur replied. "You know yourself it is much easier to be good when you have a little rice and *dal*."

Next time he came by, the old woman wouldn't take his money. He was a countryman, she said, and she wanted to treat him to tea. While he was drinking, she consulted him professionally. Her stomach was upset; did he know a true medical formula for her? When he was silent, she said, "I can pay."

"I do not need your *pice*, Grandmother," he told her. "Boil some seeds of the basil plant and drink the liquid. Bathe and say prayers regularly—and stop chewing *pan* for a week. You will recover quickly, with the gods' help."

He knew his remedy was successful because when he came for tea the third time, the tea was almost undrinkable, a sugar paste, so many teaspoonfuls of the sweetening did she drop in.

"You are doing holy work, my son," she exclaimed, and pointed Bahadur out to the only other customer, a *sanyasi* in a ragged saffron garment squatting on the side of the stall. "He is assistant to a *vaid*," she proclaimed. The *sanyasi* seemed unimpressed, but then it is hard to impress such a one.

Bahadur did not visit the place in the afternoon until the day he bought the wristwatch. Then, bathed, oiled, and carefully dressed, the watch strapped higher on his arm than most watches are worn, he strolled to the tea shop. Padmini was there, newly from her bath, clad in the very pink *sari* he had once bought for her. It was ragged now and not nearly so bright, but she was lovely as ever, her soft coppery skin like a blossom, her body small and round and full like a bursting fruit.

"Tea—" he said.

She poured, her eyes mischievous. "How are you, Doctorbabu?"

"Well. How are you?"

"I am well. But I have been sick. I had to go to clinic many days. I went first the day after you fought with Assim. My insides were very sick and I did not even know it." She looked down at the teapot steaming on the clay stove. It was the only time he had known her to be ashamed. "I did not mean to make you sick. You were very good and kind to me. Like a husband."

Now Bahadur was embarrassed. "More tea."

She poured.

"And you are all well now?"

"Well. I must not go back to clinic any more."

"And—Fat Assim lives here with you?"

"I have not been with him—or others—since that night. The government doctor told me I would be blind or crippled or I would die if I did not obey the rules. I did not want those terrible things to happen to me—so I just live here with my mother."

Her lovely face was animated now. "I looked through the glass eye of the doctor's machine and I saw all the small wiggling creatures that come into the body with the disease. I could not believe it, but the doctor said yes, those were all mine and there would be many many more that would come to make me blind if I did not take care. I have learned to be frightened—"

"Did you have shots?"

"Ai! Many many," she remembered with pleasure. "And I screamed so with all. The doctor said I was the loudest he had ever had."

He looked at her fondly. "Perhaps since you are feeling so well, you will come to the movies tonight."

She was delighted.

Bahadur has the future all planned. He will not marry but he will move in with Padmini and enjoy the pleasures of her company and her generous body. He has money and can buy her lovely presents, bangles not of glass but of various metals—possibly gold—and *saris*, until she is the best dressed woman on the road. This will content her, and she will be true to him. Otherwise, he will beat her. If a child should start within her—and she has behaved—who knows, perhaps he and she might seek a pundit and then have a marriage ceremony. He does not judge her too harshly because he knows in his heart he is no better than she. Of what use is it for the sieve to say to the needle, "You have a hole in your tail."

Bahadur writes the future in his mind with luminous ink.

They are riding toward Majumdar's village and Robi is very dissatisfied with the behavior of this ricksha-wallah. The coolie is in his debt. Recently the man came running at daybreak to lament outside Robi's door that he had acquired a dread disease. He feared it was leprosy!

"Help me!" he implored. "I have skin spots. I am being punished for a previous life of sin."

"Did I not cure you of boils—and I did that in the time before I was even a true *vaid*," Robi calmed him. "I shall examine you. Bahadur—hold the man's arm steady under the torch."

There were a few round smooth spots on the skin. No discharge.

"I can help you," Robi spoke sternly, "but this is more serious than boils. Much more serious."

"I will be your servant forever." Ram promised.

"You must follow my instructions exactly."

"I promise!"

"You may not eat flesh or drink alcohol. You must offer prayers and perform all the proper ceremonies. Cut your hair and nails short and have *no* relations with women until the spots are gone."

Bahadur prepared for Ram a medicine of ground cashew nuts well-soaked in cow's urine and milk of the cascara plant.

"Each morning after bathing you must rub this on your skin and take one dose," Robi directed. "You will, with the help of the gods, recover."

"You are my mother and my father," the grateful Ram declared, touching Robi's feet.

Ram paid only for the cost of the medicine. He gave no gifts to his benefactor, but instead he frequently lent the services of his ricksha to the medical team. The spots have not yet left the man's skin, Robi notes, and already his coolie feet move slowly.

Robi looks up at the surroundings and recognizes the place.

"You will tell the ricksha-wallah to go to the sweet shop we have only just passed a little way back," he tells Bahadur.

Bahadur is surprised. "Majumdar is having an attack. Should we not take our refreshment afterward? In the village they will provide us with drinks and sweets as always."

"The heat is oppressive today. And the dust is like pepper in my nostrils. I am feeling faint." Robi emphasizes his delicate condition by wiping his neck and brow with a fine English cambric kerchief. "I shall not be able to attend Majumdar unless I get some relief right now."

Bahadur does as he is told. "Ram, we will return to the sweet shop just past." He gestured behind them.

"But we are hurrying to Vishna—to help Majum—" The coolie cannot believe his ears.

Bahadur apprises him of the situation. "Doctorbabu is faint with the heat. He will not be able to cure the patient unless he has a drink and a rest. Doctoring is big work you know. It is not the same as pulling a ricksha."

"Let us move on to the next shop, sahibs," the ricksha-wallah urges. "It is better than the shop already gone. That shack belongs to a very old-fashioned villager. He does not even hang flypaper."

"I do not require flypaper—or any other Calcutta comforts," Robi announces to them. "This is the countryside and we are country people. Let us go to the plain shop because that is the sort of people we are, unspoiled and rustic. Simple."

Obediently, the ricksha-wallah turns around and they start back to the sweet-shop.

Glossary

Babu	*A Hindu gentleman; a title corresponding to Sir.*
Bahadur	*In India, all Nepali servants are called Bahadur. The character in this book stands for all of them.*
Biri	*A cheap, locally made cigarette.*
Charpoy	*A common light Indian cot.*
Chulha	*The common Indian word for stove usually made of mud and fired with dried cow dung.*
Dacoit	*Literally, one of a class of murderous robbers; slang for thief.*
Dal	*A sauce made of peas or other pulses.*
Dhoi	*Curds; much like yoghurt.*
Dhoti	*Flowing garment Indian men wrap around waist and legs.*
Garam Masala	*Spice used in making curry, ground fresh daily on a curry stone.*
Ghee	*Clarified or semifluid butter.*

Goala	*Milkman.*
Harijan	*Literally "child of God"; euphemism for Untouchable.*
Khadi	*Homespun cotton cloth.*
Kurta	*A long collarless shirt worn by Indian men.*
Kshatriya	*One belonging to the governing and military caste, the second of the four great Hindu castes.*
Mantra	*Popular spell or charm; ritualistic or devotional formula; hymn.*
Puja	*A religious ceremony.*
Rupee	*The monetary unit of India, made up of twelve annas or 100 pice—worth about fourteen cents (and even less today).*
Samosas	*Triangular shaped pastries stuffed with curried vegetables or meat.*
Sanyasi	*A Hindu holy man, often an itinerant begging alms.*
Seer	*A weight of about two pounds.*
Vaid	*A country doctor, practitioner of Ayurvedic medicine.*
Zamindar	*A wealthy and sometimes oppressive local landlord.*